ALSO BY TARYN SOUDERS

How to (Almost) Ruin Your Summer

COOP
KNOWS THE
SCOOP

TARYN SOUDERS

sourcebooks
young readers

To any librarian who has ever helped a reader

find the perfect book!

Published by Sourcebooks Young Readers, an imprint of Sourcebooks Kids
P.O. Box 4410, Naperville, Illinois 60567-4410
(630) 961-3900
sourcebookskids.com

Library of Congress Cataloging-in-Publication Data is on file with the publisher.

This product conforms to all applicable CPSC and CPSIA standards.

Source of Production: Versa Press, East Peoria, Illinois, USA
Date of Production: April 2022
Run Number: 5025464

Printed and bound in the United States of America.
VP 10 9 8

CHAPTER 1

WHEN THE WINDY BOTTOM TOWN council voted to tear down the old playground and build a new one, no one ever imagined what lay buried beneath the rusted slide.

The morning the human bones turned up and the news started flying around town, I was up to my ball cap in dirty coffee cups. My best friend, Justice, burst through the screened back door of A Latté Books. He slipped through spilled water on the floor and slid to a stop, clutching the counter.

"Dang it, Coop! You beat us here again."

I set a wet mug on the drying rack. "Figured if we finished our chores early, we could check out the grave. I'm dying to see the skeleton."

"Whole town's talking about it." Justice puffed out a breath of air. "Heard the police are there now."

Strangers think Jus and me are twins, because we're both cursed with messy red hair and a truckload of freckles, not to mention we're both thirteen. But his real twin is his sister Liberty, even though she looks nothing like him, being a blond and, well…a girl.

Liberty sauntered in, joining Justice and me in the kitchen. She slouched against the counter and tossed her baseball from hand to hand. Baseball was to Liberty like oxygen was to the rest of us. "That dumb ol' skeleton is all people have on their brains this morning."

"You're just mad the police won't let you on the baseball field," Justice said.

Liberty spit into the trash can. She was a southern belle. Minus the belle part.

She also ran faster and slugged harder than anyone else in Windy Bottom. "It's probably just some soldier left over from the Civil War."

Justice tied on an apron and grabbed a tub filled with dirty dishes. "Nuh-uh. Dad said there wasn't hardly any war fought in this part of Georgia."

Liberty rolled her eyes. "That doesn't mean there was *nothing*. Maybe he crawled home to die."

"Come on, Lib," I said, tossing her an apron. "We all got kitchen duty—not just Justice and me."

"I've never seen a skeleton before," Justice said. "The one hanging in Grupe's class don't count."

"Doesn't count," Liberty corrected. Ignoring his glare, she stood straight and shoved her baseball into her apron pocket. "And it's too late. No one can get within a hundred feet of the playground." She frowned. "Or the baseball fields. The police already cordoned off the whole area."

Justice sighed. "Does *cordoned* start with a *k* or a *c*?"

"*C*," Liberty and I answered together.

Justice muttered and reached for his now dog-eared pocket dictionary. Liberty threw out vocabulary the same way she threw a fastball—smooth and unstoppable. Three years ago Justice started carrying a dictionary in his back pocket after an unfortunate misunderstanding of the word "rendezvous" left him locked in the women's bathroom of the Piggly Wiggly for two hours.

I thought Jus was destined to spend his life one step behind in every conversation on account of him having to look up words so often, but Gramps said Jus may well pass us all with his vocabulary one day. According to Gramps, life is a journey, and what we are now is not necessarily what we will be.

Justice sighed. "Well, at least we could see what the police are doing. Take some pictures maybe?"

Mama poked her head through the kitchen door and smiled at the twins. "Hi, Jus. Lib. Do y'all mind watching the counter for a while? The coffee delivery came in along with a bunch of book orders. Your folks and I need to run inventory."

A couple years ago Liberty and Justice's folks, Mr. and Mrs. Gordon, owned the used bookstore next door. They must've tired out their imaginations giving their kids creative names because their store had just been called Used Books.

But then that all changed. The inside wall between mama's coffee shop and their bookstore had been demolished and A Latté Books, Windy Bottom's first and only bookstore café—with new books, not just used ones—was where Lib, Jus, and I spent our summers. Us kids got stuck washing dishes, shelving books, or whatever else needed doing.

Jus rubbed the back of his neck. "Actually ma'am, we were just about to go to the—"

I kicked him.

Mama raised her eyebrows and stepped inside, letting the swinging door *thlop* back and forth behind her. "Cooper Goodman," she poked me with her clipboard. "You're up to something, and if you think that 'something' happens to involve the skeleton at the playground, then you've got another thing coming. The store is brimming over with people, and I need your help."

Where was Gramps when I needed him? He would've let us go—in fact, I reckon he would've even given us a ride to the playground. He might be a stickler for the rules, but he had his mischievous side too.

The bell dinged at the coffee counter. Mama glanced out the small rectangular window that was set in the kitchen door. "It's Meriwether and Ruth."

Checking the time on her watch, she sighed. "I have to go." She turned to leave but stopped and nodded at the two sisters standing at the counter. "Don't forget you'll need to bring them their order. Lord knows we don't want them trying to carry their coffee again. Not after yesterday's fiasco."

"Yes, ma'am."

"Gramps will be in later on to help. But right now, sugar, I need you not distracted by talk of a skeleton." She patted my cheek.

"Ma," I whispered. Sugar's a wimpy name, and I'd told her a million times.

Lib snorted.

Mama smiled. "I'm sorry. And Coop," Mama put her hand on her hip and shook her finger. "Stay *here*. The police don't need anyone underfoot."

My shoulders sagged. "I promise."

CHAPTER 2

LIBERTY AND JUSTICE FOLLOWED ME through the swinging kitchen door to the front where whitewashed brick walls, overloaded bookcases, and hardwood floors the color of roasted coffee beans greeted us. One perk of being the only bookstore café in Windy Bottom was everyone came there to talk and drink. Then talk some more. Then a little bit more. Plus, owing to the fact that a dead body just got itself uncovered, the place was full of people needing to caffeinate their shock back down to acceptable levels of chitchat.

If I couldn't go near the site, the next best place to gather information was at A Latté Books eavesdropping on Ruth and Meriwether Feather, who were waiting for their coffee at the counter. Their skills in gathering and spreading gossip were unsurpassed in Tipton County. If you ever wanted news to travel fast, you just had to give it to the Feather sisters and make it sound like a secret—they couldn't keep their mouths shut even if their lips were hog-tied.

The Feather sisters were teachers and had taught everyone in Windy Bottom for the past hundred years, or close to it. Between the two of them, they knew the history of the whole town. They had retired from teaching a few years back due to "illness." Said they were sick of the school, and the school was sick of them.

Jus told me he was pretty sure he suffered from the same disease.

"Look at those two." Liberty nudged me and gestured with her head toward Miss Ruth and Miss Meriwether. "They look like a pair of jays with their chittering and chattering."

Both wore hats with a sprout of blue feathers on the side, reminding me that today was Thursday. They'd assigned a different color feather for each day of the week.

I whispered to Justice, "How 'bout you and Lib wipe down tables? Try to listen in on people's conversations. Bet you they're talking about that skeleton."

I rubbed my hands down the front of my jeans to dry any dishwater from them and walked to where the Feather sisters leaned against the counter. "The usual, ladies?"

Miss Ruth smiled. "Does a hound dog hunt?"

I mustered up the most charm possible for any thirteen-year-old boy stuck behind a counter serving coffee when a perfectly good skeleton lay in a shallow grave just a couple miles over. "I like the blue feather, Miss Ruth. Is that a different shade from last Thursday's?"

She adjusted the tilt of her hat. "Sure is." Only she said it like *shore is*. Miss Ruth had a low singsongy voice that could've relaxed the curls on her head if Burma from the Cut 'N' Curl hadn't wrapped the rods so tight during her last perm—Liberty's words, not mine.

"And you should see the fine-looking orange color we've got picked out for Tuesday. Downright cheerful. The last one was becoming disrespectfully shabby."

"Oh muzzle it, Ruth." Miss Meriwether didn't bother looking up. She didn't have to in order for me to know she was scowling. She always was. Miss Ruth constantly smiled and had mischievous eyes, but Miss Meriwether had scowl gutters that ran deep, making her face look like that picture of Winston Churchill that hung in the library—which was pretty unnerving considering she wasn't a man. "The feather wasn't shabby. It was acceptable."

Mama said some people ease their way into a cranky lifestyle, but not Miss Meriwether. She cannonballed right into a swamp of cantankerousness and has been treading the murky water ever since.

"Besides, Cooper doesn't want to hear you gab on about colors, you silly old crow."

"It's just Coop, Miss Meriwether, ma'am," I said. "The *er* is silent, remember?"

Miss Meriwether peered over the counter and watched as I poured coffee into the teacups in front of me. She had an intense dislike of mugs. Thought they were uncouth. Said one could slurp mud from a teacup and be more refined than being seen drinking coffee out of a mug.

Her beady eyes bored holes through my head. "Do you remember I don't want any of that artificial sweetener junk?"

"Yes, ma'am."

"I like the fake stuff," said Miss Ruth with a grin.

And I liked Miss Ruth. She was like the grandma I never had.

"None of that garbage for you, sister. It's not good for you. And where's your sweater? You'll catch a chill."

"It's eighty-eight degrees outside, Meriwether. I declare, you could start an argument in an empty house." Miss Ruth winked at me. "Don't be such a sourpuss."

Miss Meriwether made a sound like she was sucking her teeth and muttered something about cold air-conditioning and catching the flu.

I rang them up on the cash register. "I'll bring y'all's drinks to you. Still sitting next to Biographies?" I said, placing their coffee-filled teacups on a tray.

Miss Ruth nodded and patted my hand. "Such a honey bee."

Another wimpy name. At least Gramps never called me anything embarrassing.

I took my time adding napkins, sugar packets, and creamers to the tray in order to give them a head start. Then I navigated my way through a maze of narrow aisles created by the floor-to-ceiling bookshelves to get to Biographies, where Miss Meriwether and Miss Ruth sat in overstuffed armchairs waiting for their coffee.

I set the tray on the side table wedged between their chairs and then played my hand.

"So… I've been in the kitchen all morning. Anything new in town?"

Miss Meriwether gawked. "Cooper Goodman, do you mean to tell me you haven't heard?"

"Excuse me, ma'am, but the *er* is—"

Miss Ruth pulled on my arm. "They've found a body at the old playground—a *skeleton*."

I didn't pump my fist, but I wanted to. Here it was. The good, the bad, and the gossip.

"I heard," she whispered, "from Ms. Millie, who overheard Suds tell Wendell, that one of the construction workers told him that"—she paused dramatically and looked around before continuing—"the skeleton was wearing a dress!"

Miss Meriwether's teacup rattled in its saucer.

"It's a girl skeleton?" I wondered if Justice and Liberty had heard *that* tidbit yet.

Like Justice, I'd never seen a *real* skeleton, much less one in a dress. The one in Miss Grupe's class was made of plastic. We called it Dead Fred, and the closest it ever came to having a wardrobe was at Christmas time when Miss Grupe plopped a Santa hat on its bony skull.

I squatted down eye level with them. "Any idea who it was?"

Miss Ruth shook her head. "No one's been murdered here for quite some time."

The eyeglasses perched on the tip of Miss Meriwether's nose fell off. "Mother of Abraham Lincoln! Who said anything about murder, Ruth?" She huffed. "The playground's probably just an old family burial site." She shook her head and scowled. "Such nonsense."

Miss Ruth patted my hand. "Don't you be worried about getting yourself murdered too, Coop, dear." She took a sip of coffee. "I'm sure we're all safe."

I returned to the counter and motioned Liberty and Justice to meet me.

I told them about the dress.

Justice nudged Liberty. "See? Told ya. You ever heard of a Civil War soldier wearing a dress? I sure ain't."

She rammed her hand into her apron pocket, pulled out her baseball, and considered the question. Dresses were to Liberty like brussels sprouts were to most of humanity—the God-fearing portion at least.

"More likely to find a soldier wearing a dress than *me*."

CHAPTER 3

THE CRUNCH OF GRAVEL PULLED my attention away from the coffee counter. Through the store's front windows sunlight glinted off a dark blue sedan. TIPTON COUNTY SHERIFF was emblazoned on the side of the doors. To everyone else, he was Deputy Keith Vidler, but to me he was Tick.

Justice nudged me. "The sheriff's office."

"You have a prodigious grasp of the obvious," muttered Liberty.

Justice reached for his dictionary.

I rolled my eyes. "She means amazing, and she's also being sarcastic."

We weren't the only ones who'd noticed his arrival. Chair legs scraped against the old wooden floor, and tabletops jostled as people rushed to the front of the store to spy through the windows. Faces and hands pressed against the once-clean glass panes—panes that yours truly would have to wipe down. Tick unfolded himself out of his squad car, tucked a pair of sunglasses into the front pocket of his starched uniform, and put his hat on. How someone his height ever managed to fit inside any car boggled my mind.

Tick used to pitch for the Atlanta Braves until he threw out his shoulder. So he traded his glove for a holster and came back to his hometown.

One might have thought our fire alarm had gone off the way folks poured out the door and crowded around him, pelting him with questions. Tick would've gone to meet his Maker right then and there if those questions had been bullets. I stood with my feet just inside the doorway so if Mama asked I could tell her honestly I never left the store.

"What's the word on the body?"

"Who is it?"

"How long's it been there?"

"Where's Chief Rogers?"

"Hey, Keith! Was it murder?"

"When can we play baseball again?"

Everyone turned and stared at Liberty, who stood at the top of the steps, tossing her ball.

"What?" She shrugged. "We've got a game coming up."

I don't care what Gramps said about how life was a journey and how there were always forks in the road we could take to change our direction. I was pretty sure Lib's road was going to take her straight to being the first female player in the big leagues. She was a good player, but talent wouldn't get her onto a team. Sheer cussedness would. She was the most stubborn girl ever. Danced to her own tune, Mama said. Ha! As if Lib would ever be caught dead dancing.

Tick grinned. "Your batting average is already better than mine, Liberty." He held up his hands to the crowd. "I can't talk about an ongoing investigation. As soon as I have something I'm able to give y'all, I will. You got my word. Now back inside—your coffees are getting cold."

He shooed people in the direction of the door. "Plus, you're blocking the sidewalk."

"That's the least of your problems now, Vidler," someone shouted.

Tick shook his head and dragged himself up the steps to where I stood.

"Morning, Coop." He took his hat off. "Your mama in?"

I thumbed toward the back hallway. "In the storeroom doing inventory."

He smiled and gave me a small salute. "Thank you."

When Mama and I moved in with Gramps after Daddy's

death, Tick was the first to appear on the front porch, welcoming us. Daddy and Tick had been best friends growing up. He told me stories of him and Daddy getting in all sorts of trouble. Stories that helped both Mama and I crawl out from underneath our sadness. "We were inseparable," Tick said. "People would say if your daddy was a hound dog, then I was the tick." It had been the first time in ages I'd laughed at something, so after that, he told me I could call him *Tick* if I wanted. I was eight years old, and I'd been calling him that ever since.

I stepped in front of him and stood straight, trying to gain an inch of height. "So you really don't know who you dug up?"

Liberty nudged me aside. "We know it's a lady though, right? I mean, the skeleton was in a dress." She tightened her lips. "Though personally, I wouldn't be caught dead in one."

Tick sighed. "How'd you hear about that?"

"We got connections."

Mama popped around the corner, holding her clipboard. "Wondered if that was you causing such a ruckus, Keith. We heard it all the way back in the storeroom."

Tick admitted to his ruckus-causing with a nod. "Guilty as charged."

"Are you investigating that mess up at the playground?"

"Sure am."

"What's the Tipton County Sheriff's office doing getting

their hands dirty with this? Not that I object, mind you." She tapped her pencil against his wide shoulder and smiled. "But the playground is within the Windy Bottom township."

He nodded. "Chief Rogers asked. Said it's just her right now. She feels like she's treading in a mud pit and could use the help." He ran his fingers around the rim of his hat. "Not an easy thing for a police chief to ask. Got to admire her for that."

Mama nodded. "Murray left yesterday for a two-week cruise with his new bride. And O'Connell just had his appendix out. No wonder she feels overwhelmed."

"The sheriff figured since I live here I'll have an easier go at things."

She studied him for a moment and a smile crept across her lips. "You look like you got trampled by a herd of cattle."

He grinned and rubbed the back of his neck. "Nope—just your customers."

"Let's get you some coffee. Then I'll show you a quiet spot near Poetry where you can set yourself down and think. Or get some shut-eye." She winked at him.

"A nap would be nice, but I need to make a few calls. Couldn't get a decent signal at the playground."

He placed his hand on her back and followed her.

Jus elbowed me and gestured toward Tick and Mama as they disappeared down the hall. "Whoa. What's up with that?"

"Where've you been? He's been sweet on her for months."

Justice turned to me, eyes wide. "She like him back?"

I rubbed the back of my neck. "I overheard her tell Gramps she's a sucker for a guy in uniform."

Daddy had died five years ago, and I knew Mama was lonely. But Tick? I liked him a lot, but a policeman's job could be just as dangerous as the Marines. What if something happened? Mama didn't need to go through all that again.

Neither did I.

CHAPTER 4

BURMA MOSEYED INTO OUR STORE moments later, gray hair slicked back and smelling of aftershave. He ran the Cut 'N' Curl and owned three things that half the people in town didn't: all his teeth, a full head of hair, and a sense of humor. He had years of experience pulling pranks.

"Morning, Coop." He leaned against the counter and thumbed behind him toward the door. "Saw the deputy pull in. Is he here for me?" He chuckled at his own joke.

"Only if you mess up Shakespeare again," Liberty muttered. She handed me a clean mug for Burma's drink then focused her stare on him. "We're under strict orders from Mom to keep an eye on you."

Last week he took it upon himself to rearrange all of Shakespeare's tragedies based on how the main character kicked the bucket. It took Liberty and Mrs. Gordon ages before the books went from *stabbed*, *poisoned*, or *baked into a pie* (that one's from *Titus Andronicus*), back to alphabetical order.

I slid his latté across the counter and looked around to make sure Mama wasn't nearby. "Hey, Burma. Have you gone up to the playground? Do you know anything about the skeleton? Mama won't let us check it out."

He shook his head. "Sorry, son. I'm staying out of the way. Besides, I don't need to go looking for news. News tends to walk right through the front door of my shop and make itself comfortable in the chairs." He chuckled and paid for his coffee. "You know how it is."

I might as well have tossed my hopes alongside the coffee beans Liberty was pouring into the grinder.

He eyeballed my head. "Speaking of... You're looking shaggier than a stray dog."

I ran my fingers through my hair with a slim hope it would look less wild.

Burma shook his head. "Now you've gone and made it worse. But if I know your mama, she'll have you come in to see me before school starts."

She probably would.

"Harley in yet? I want to ask him about this wart on my finger."

I shook my head. "Should be in soon."

Harley was my gramps. And before he retired and became the town philosopher—as Mama called him—he had been the town doctor. He'd spent plenty of time both bringing people into the world and seeing them out of it. Most everyone still called him Doc. Mama and Burma were the only ones who called him by his actual name. Probably 'cause Burma and Gramps had been friends since they were kids.

Burma leaned in. The scent of his aftershave floated over the counter. "Is my Ruth flower here?"

Justice, with a dish towel draped over his shoulder, pushed a tray stacked with dirty coffee mugs and crumb-filled plates across the counter toward me. "Don't you mean feather? Ruth Feather? She's here. Her sister too."

Burma grinned at him. "No, son. I mean my *flower*." Then he winked.

From the doorway, Liberty caught my eye and pointed her finger down her throat, pretending to gag. Justice's brow wrinkled in confusion.

"Romance befuddles him even more than vocabulary, Burma," I said. "His brain misfired one day in the fourth grade after we watched a video on puberty."

Liberty snickered. "Yeah. I think the idea a girl might like him one day scared him near to stupid. I told him that was something he shouldn't ever worry about though."

Burma's eyes twinkled. "I see."

"Miss Ruth and Miss Meriwether sat down a few minutes ago—just before Tick arrived," I said. "They're in their usual spot, talking about the skeleton probably. Miss Meriwether seems to be not-so-merry today," I warned.

"Crankier than usual, eh?" He grabbed Mama's small vase of fresh cut flowers that sat next to the cash register, then hurried off to join the Feather sisters.

A half hour later Liberty, Justice, and I circulated the bookstore wiping down tables and straightening chairs. Apparently, since Tick hadn't shared anything of interest, the morning crowd had taken it upon themselves to witness the to-do at the playground firsthand, leaving a path of empty chairs and lipstick-stained cups wider than Sherman's March to the Sea. No doubt Lib, Jus, and I were the only ones in town *not* at the playground.

I dropped Miss Meriwether's, Miss Ruth's, and Burma's empty dishes onto my tray with a clatter. A teacup rattled in its saucer and threatened to tip over but didn't. I picked up the tiny vase and plopped it down too.

Daddy had always been a stickler for duty—probably got it from Gramps. But I bet *he* would've left the dishes and cut out to see a skeleton…maybe.

I sighed. No, he wouldn't. Not if he'd already said he'd help Mama. He had been a man of his word. Mama and Gramps and Tick all told me that.

I spun around and collided into Tick.

"Whoa there, Coop." The vase toppled into his hands. "Sorry—wasn't expecting you to turn around so quickly." He stared at the vase before setting it back on my tray. "Your flowers are missing."

"Burma." I figured that was explanation enough.

"Ah. Hey, if I dropped off a poster for the clothing drive the police are sponsoring, would you tape it somewhere it'd be seen?"

"Sure."

His hands rested on his holster belt and he looked at my tray full of cups and plates. "You do a good job helping your mama, Coop. Your daddy would've been proud of you."

I looked away. "I suppose so."

He grabbed my shoulder. "Oh no, you don't. What's wrong? You don't think your daddy would be proud?"

I shrugged. "Let's face it. Doing dishes and shelving books at the café hardly screams heroic. It's not even close to being like a Marine."

Tick leaned against the bookcase and crossed his arms. "Two things, Coop."

I looked at him.

He held up a finger. "One—there are no thirteen-year-old Marine heroes in the world. Cut yourself some slack."

I smiled. Yeah. Maybe. I guess even Daddy wasn't a Marine hero when he was my age.

"Two," Tick said, holding up another finger. "Your dad had his talents, and you have your own. You're the best problem solver I've met. You've got a good, logical brain. Your mama tells me you designed a new inventory-tracking spreadsheet."

"Yeah, well, that was just so I didn't have to waste my whole summer using that old system she had."

Tick shook his head. "The reason doesn't matter. You're a talented kid and on your way to being a great man, Coop. Give yourself time. And believe me when I say you *have* done your daddy proud." He smiled. "Now, tell me you believe me, so I can get my coffee and get back to work."

"Okay, fine. I believe you," I said.

Tick stepped back to let me through and followed me to the counter. "I need to order some coffee for the team at the crime scene. I'm about to head back." He pulled out his wallet.

I shook my head. "You know Mama's rules. Anyone in uniform gets free coffee—pretty sure that includes your CSI team. You'll get me grounded."

He smiled. "I doubt that. But to be on the safe side, we'll do it your way." He pulled out a twenty, stuffed it in the tip jar next to the register, and winked at me. "Your mama never said anything about not tipping the help, though."

Justice came back from his station by the front window—where he'd been pretending to wash tables while he peered down the street in the direction of the playground—and peeked into the normally empty jar. "Wow! Sweet! Thanks, Deputy."

I circled around the counter and checked the level of coffee. "I'll need to grind more beans. It's going to take a few minutes." I turned my head toward the kitchen. "Hey, Lib! Bring out some beans, will ya?"

Tick checked his watch and frowned.

Inspiration hit like a blast of air-conditioning. "Tell you what, Tick. Since you're obviously in a hurry and this'll take some time, why don't you head out? I got an idea."

The swinging door *thwopped* back and forth, and Liberty plopped a large bag of unground coffee beans on the counter.

I stepped on Lib's foot, signaling her to stick around. "Mr. Gordon installed delivery baskets on our bikes a couple weeks back. Give us time to brew a jug of joe, and we'll bring it with all the fixings over to y'all at the playground." I looked at the clock behind the register. "It might not be until around eleven that we make it there. Will that be too late for coffee?"

"It's never too late for coffee, Coop. Ask any police officer." Tick grinned. "But doesn't your mama need you in the shop?"

Mama had wanted our help that morning, but now that she'd had time to get some work done, maybe we could cut loose. As if divinely directed, Gramps walked through the swinging door of the kitchen.

"Hey, Coop." He squeezed my shoulder.

Gramps was tall and strong, just like Daddy had been, though Tick stood a good three inches taller. He dished out the kind of hugs that stayed with you for an entire day. Gramps pulled an apron over his head of hair that refused to turn gray and nodded a greeting to Tick.

"Gramps! Perfect timing." I smiled casually. "Can you watch over the place? We got an important errand for Tick."

"Please, Doc," Justice said. "We're dying to see—"

I stomped on his foot.

"—how well the delivery baskets work."

A small frown creased his forehead. "Hold on, son. You check with your mama?"

There was nothing for it. I headed for the back room. Clutching the doorframe, I explained our plan. "Please, Mama. Gramps is here." I took a deep breath. I didn't want to sound whiny. Goodmans don't whine—I remembered that from Daddy too. "We won't cause any trouble. I promise."

She narrowed her eyes. "You best not get underfoot. You take the coffee over, set stuff up, and come straight back, you hear?"

"Yes, ma'am! Thank you!" I left before she could change her mind.

"And Coop?"

I stopped and turned. "Ma'am?"

She poked her head out the storeroom door. "I know everyone's curious, but remember it's a grave." Her eyes held a hint of sadness. "Show respect for the dead."

CHAPTER 5

LIB, JUS, AND I ARRIVED at the playground with three large jugs filled with hot coffee in our baskets, along with a bag stuffed with cups, sugar, and creamers.

"Sheesh." Liberty balanced a jug on her hip and dropped her bike to the dirt. "The whole town's here."

"I bet Dollar Daze is closed for the morning—there's Mr. Ponti." I nodded toward where Mr. Ponti chattered with Willy the postman. "And it looks like no one's getting mail."

"Nobody's getting any gas, either," said Justice.

Suds O'Leary, owner of Windy Bottom Gas and Bait, and the Feather sisters huddled together in conversation in a prime observation spot near the front of the crowd. You could pick Suds out of a crowd a mile away. In a not-so-brilliant marketing move, he'd ordered two hundred puke-green T-shirts plastered with the phrase "SUDS GAVE ME GAS." He'd said he hoped to "improve his market visibility" by selling them. He was visible, all right. But he was the only one who ever wore them.

Even the bank manager, Mr. Rutherford Willis, surrendered to curiosity about the crime scene. Sure it was a sweltering ninety-five degrees in the shade, but he still wore a three-piece suit. I elbowed Liberty and pointed toward where he leaned against the side of his shimmering black Cadillac, silk tie and all. She rolled her eyes and snorted.

We pushed our way through the crowd of onlookers who waited outside the black-and-yellow-striped crime scene tape surrounding the area around the playground.

The playground was crawling with crime scene investigators in white jumpsuits. A TIPTON COUNTY CRIME SCENE UNIT van was parked near the construction trailer. The investigators were sifting through dirt, taking photos, or writing on clipboards. One CSI dumped shovelfuls of dirt from inside the excavator's large scoop into a shallow box while another person gently shook the box back and forth, allowing the dirt to fall through the holes. Someone else put a soil sample into an evidence bag and sealed it with tape.

Justice frowned. "What do you think they're looking for?"

Liberty came up behind him. "Probably evidence of some kind. Let's get a closer look."

Tick stood talking with another police officer near an excavator. I handed over my coffee jug to Justice and whistled. Tick looked up and waved.

Justice handed me back the coffee. "Do you think that's the excavator that uncovered the skeleton?"

"Hope so." I grinned. "That'd be cool."

Suds O'Leary waved us over to where he stood near the front of crowd. "Make room now, folks."

"Coming through! We got an important delivery!"

Most of the customers from A Latté Books, along with several other town folks, craned their necks and stood on their toes to see what was happening. I set my jug of coffee on the ground and placed my feet on either side to make sure no one kicked it over.

Large, odd-shaped pieces of the old slide, the merry-go-round, and the jungle gym stuck out the top of the beat-up dumpster in the weed-infested lot. They looked like giant metal ants trying to crawl over the edge of the container.

The only piece of equipment still standing was the swing set. But to say it was standing would be a lie bigger than Suds O'Leary's waistline. Its rusted frame leaned at a precarious angle, threatening to collapse any second like a bad game of Jenga.

Liberty let out a long, low whistle. "This place is a wreck."

"Darn tootin'!" said Suds, his T-shirt stretched over his belly, emphasizing the word "gas." As much as I wanted to focus on the scene in front of me, bizarrely all I could think was that a man wearing a shirt with the word "gas" on it probably shouldn't be using phrases with "tootin'" in them.

Large pits puckered the ground from where the old equipment once stood. But the hole that grabbed everyone's attention and held it hostage was the one where the slide used to sit.

Liberty jostled against me as someone wiggled his way between her and Justice.

"Hey, watch the coffee!" I said.

A tall sweaty kid turned around and grinned. "My bad, Coop. Didn't see it." He elbowed Lib. "What'd I miss?"

"Hey, Ambrose. By the smell of you, I'd say you missed a shower." She wrinkled her nose. "Where've you been?"

He swiped a trail of sweat from his forehead and looked at his hand before wiping it on his shorts. "I heard about the skeleton while I was cutting the lawn. Dumb mower ran out of gas halfway through, so it took longer than I wanted. Didn't bother showering, because I was afraid I'd miss something." He sniffed his armpit. "It's not that bad."

"Says you," muttered Lib.

In a stroke of genius that was out of character for him, he had brought binoculars. A jolt of jealousy poked me as he lifted them to his eyes.

I nudged him. "Can I see, Ambrose? Please?"

"Won't do you any good." He brought the binoculars down and swiped his hair out of his eyes. "That stupid pile of dirt is in the way—can't see diddly-squat."

Justice huffed. "The police should be more solicitous and move the dirt to the other side." He leaned over and grinned. "I learned *that* word last week."

"Ambrose," I stepped toward him. "Let me climb on your shoulders."

"What?"

"Come on—it's the only way we'll see anything. You're the tallest one here."

He was the tallest kid in class last year too—mainly because Ambrose liked sixth grade so much he decided to enjoy it twice.

Ambrose scowled. "How about Liberty? She weighs less."

I could tell a part of Liberty was sorely tempted to have a go at those binoculars, but then she sniffed the air near him and grimaced. "Not happening."

"Shucks." Ambrose sighed and handed the binoculars to Justice. "Hold these for a minute." He bent down.

I held Justice's shoulders as I climbed onto Ambrose. "Okay—I'm on. Don't drop me."

Ambrose clasped his hands around my calves and slowly straightened.

I wobbled but stayed upright. "Hand me the binoculars, Jus."

Justice held them up. I draped the strap over my neck and peered through the lenses.

"Well?" Ambrose said. "What do you see?"

I fiddled with the focus nob. "There's a guy in the hole. The back of his coverall says Medical Examiner."

"It's a grave, not a hole," Justice said.

Ambrose shifted suddenly to the left. I dropped the binoculars and grabbed his head. "Quit moving!"

"Sorry. Something was crawling on my leg."

"Don't be a sissy, Ambrose," Liberty said, with a hint of disgust. "It was just sweat."

I pulled the binoculars up and peered through them again. "Okay… The guy is waving Tick over… Tick's coming…he's… he's handing Tick…wait a minute…" I focused in more.

Dead silence fell over the crowd as they listened to me.

Gold briefly glinted in the sunlight.

"It looks like a piece of jewelry," I said.

The crowd murmured.

"A dress and jewelry," Liberty muttered. "Trust a Yank to get gussied up for battle."

Tick held the item up for closer examination, and then he took a photo with his phone. After that, he slid the item into an evidence bag and marked it.

Ambrose tilted his head toward me. "What else do you see?"

I lifted the binoculars back up. "Hold on... There's something."

The crowd fell silent again.

"Bones! He's handing up bones, and they're being put in a body bag!" I dropped the binoculars.

Mama and I lived with Gramps in the same house Daddy had grown up in. After Daddy died a few years back, Mama wanted to raise me near family. Gramps invited us to Windy Bottom. Mama's own folks were missionaries in Papua New Guinea, and I guess she figured moving us to Georgia would be an easier transition than the jungle.

The three of us formed a new family, trying to fill the craters in our hearts left by the space Daddy used to fill. Gramps stepped in where Daddy should've been, and, more and more, he was becoming a dad to me. I knew that I could depend on him and that he loved me.

He was as trustworthy as the sunrise. It was Gramps who'd taught me how to catch trout down at Plotter's Creek and Liberty's fastballs at the baseball field. It was Gramps who stayed home with me when I was sick and Mama was working. It was Gramps who cooked dinner half the time. And it was Gramps who explained girls to me—as much as *he* understood, anyway.

He had only two rules: don't drink and don't gamble. The rules weren't a problem, as long as Gramps wasn't suggesting root beer was a bad thing.

Mama held out a glass of iced tea. "Coop, sugar, will you take Gramps his tea while I finish heating up dinner?" She swiped a strand of long hair out of her face.

I took the sweating glass from Mama's hand and wandered down the hall to the living room. Aside from the sun coming up and going down, fewer things were more certain than finding Gramps in his favorite recliner each night reading the local paper, the *Windy Bottom Breeze*, and sipping iced tea so sweet it'd make your teeth hurt. I set the glass on the side table next to him.

He folded the *Windy Bottom Breeze* and dropped it to the floor. The special evening edition headline read "Mysterious Skeleton Uncovered in Windy Bottom!"

I picked the paper up and tucked it under my arm, with plans to scour the pages for information later. "At least Earl will have something to do other than trying to bury poor Chester before he's actually dead," I said.

Earl's family had owned and operated Comforted Souls Funeral Parlor since the first Windy Bottom citizen bit the dust back in 1848. For years, Earl Winston kept alive the tradition of consoling people recently deprived of a loved one. It was the *only* thing kept alive under his care. And oddly enough, for a man who was extremely claustrophobic, he spent all his time closing people up in tight spaces. He had accidently gotten himself trapped in one of the coffins in the showroom when he was kid. Suffice it to say he didn't rest in peace.

Gramps looked up from his tea. "Bury Chester? What are you talking about? That dog's not dead."

I sat on the sofa across from him. "Thought you heard about it. Last Tuesday, that dumb Doberman gulped down a rotten veggie omelet he'd sniffed out near the dumpster. He spent the afternoon regretting the experience. I don't know if it was because the omelet was five days old, or 'cause it had vegetables, but Earl found him passed out in the alley. I guess he must've looked dead, 'cause Earl stuck him in his hearse and made for the cemetery for a doggie funeral."

Gramps laughed.

"But Chester got him back—he came to and puked all over the navy blue upholstery."

"That old fool. You'd think he'd be able to tell the difference between living and dead."

"Man, you should have heard him screaming at Jus and Lib, 'I'm going to be smelling dog puke from now until next year, blah, blah, blah. It's not like I have another car to drive...blah, blah, blah.' His face turned three different shades of purple. Spit was flying from his mouth. It's not Jus and Lib's fault Earl doesn't have another car and that he uses that hearse to run all his errands. He should learn to take a pulse."

Gramps shook his head. "It's messed up. Him packing his milk and eggs in the back of the car one week, and then sliding a coffin in the next. It feels somehow disrespectful to the dearly departed."

"Well, luckily the dead don't know the difference, so that's one good thing."

He laughed. "And they can't smell, either, so that's the second good thing. There you go, Coop. You may take your leave."

Oh yeah, I forgot. Gramps had a third rule: You can't leave a bad situation without finding two good things about it. Two things to be thankful for.

"One more good thing, as bonus," he said as I was about out the door. I turned. "It makes for a hilarious story. Chester puking in the hearse. Now *that's* funny."

CHAPTER 6

THE SUN ROSE FRIDAY MORNING, bringing with it a bucket-load of unanswered questions I had about the skeleton. As Lib, Jus, and I pedaled into the town square, the digital clock on the bank's sign flipped to eight-zero-something. That was because the last digit had burned out sometime before I was born. But it didn't matter. One could tell time by just knowing the routines of the citizens of Windy Bottom.

Tick bounded up the steps of A Latté Books. Perfect timing! I raced into the alley, sending a spray of loose gravel in the direction of the dumpster. Liberty and Justice were on my tail, but I took great satisfaction in being the first through the back door of the kitchen.

Gramps stood with his back to me, stacking a rack of mugs.

"Morning, Gramps." I tried to dash past.

But he caught me and wrapped me in a hug. "Coop! Where's the fire?"

I struggled against him, but Gramps was as strong as black coffee. "I want to talk to Tick," I garbled into his shirt. He smelled of lemon soap and coffee beans, a strange combination, but one I loved because it reminded me of him.

He chuckled and held me out at arm's length. "Not before a morning hug."

Liberty burst through the screen door with Justice at her heels. She wiped a bead of sweat from the side of her face.

"I got to run, Gramps."

I broke free and pushed through the swinging kitchen door into the café.

"Where's Tick, Mama?" I asked.

"And good morning to you too." Mama looked over her shoulder as she poured coffee beans into a latté machine. "Cutting it kind of close to opening time, don't you think?"

Justice nodded. "My bike tire was flatter than a snake run over by a tractor. I had to fix it. Didn't even get a chance to eat breakfast."

"The pastry order hasn't been delivered yet, but you can grab one of Earl's muffins from the kitchen."

Justice wrinkled his nose. "I'll go hungry," he mumbled.

For as long as I can remember, Earl had brought muffins to the bookstore about once a week. He said it was because he's always loved baking, but I think he was secretly hoping Mama would sell his stuff in the café. Problem was, the stench of formaldehyde hung around anything he came near, including his muffins. It was impossible to eat something that smelled like death. Plus, I'm pretty sure the health department would have a problem with food deliveries being made in the back of a hearse—especially one that now smelled like dog vomit.

"Mama," I said. "I saw you let Tick in early and I just... wondered if he knew anything."

"I'm sure he knows a lot of things, Coop. But let me tell you what I know." She faced us. "Y'all aren't the only ones who noticed Keith pull up out front. The morning crowd will pour in faster than I can say 'maximum occupancy exceeded' when I unlock those front doors. Which means the three of you need to get ready to help out." She turned, grabbed three aprons, and tossed one to each of us. "Jus and Lib, your folks volunteered you to help out at the counter this morning. Oh! And Coop" —she pointed over my shoulder—"Keith dropped off that poster by the register. Said something about you hanging it up for him?"

Oh yeah. The clothing drive. I'd forgotten.

"And don't forget it's Friday."

Two years ago, Mama had volunteered my services as lawn

boy to the Feather sisters after she overheard them fussing over their too-small teachers' pensions and the price of yard care. Fridays were my day to wrestle with Ol' Feisty—their angst-filled lawn mower—for a measly five dollars.

True to form, Mama was right—the caffeine flowed like the Chattahoochee River at flood stage. Even if I'd wanted to take the time to find Tick and pelt him with all my questions, Mama kept me running with coffee orders, wiping down tables, and cleaning dirty dishes. It wasn't until maybe an hour had flown by that Tick snuck up on me as I straightened the books in the Biographies section.

"Hey, Coop."

I spun around. "Tick! Where've you been?"

He put his finger to his lips and peeked around the bookshelf to the front of the bookstore. The cushioned chairs and sofas were filled with people discussing what they'd witnessed at the playground the day before. And if they weren't talking about what *they* saw or heard, they gabbed on about what their neighbor saw or heard.

"Hiding in the back room. I needed to jot down some notes in peace and quiet. By the way, thanks for hanging the poster and a double thanks for bringing the coffee to us yesterday."

"Thanks for letting us come." I looked over my shoulder and checked for Mama. She had a sixth sense when I wasn't doing what I was supposed to do and could appear out of nowhere. "So listen, Tick. I've got a few questions I—"

"Walk and talk." He gestured toward the counter with an empty mug. "I need more coffee."

I shook my head. "Bad idea. You'll get yourself buried under an avalanche of questions if anyone out there sees you."

"One of the many hazards of my job," he said taking a step.

I pushed him back into the aisle. "Wait. Gramps has a shirt in the office. Let me grab it for you so at least your uniform isn't so dang obvious."

Tick grinned. "I like how you think, Coop."

I dashed down the hall, and moments later Tick slipped his big arms into the long flannel sleeves, but didn't button it. It was a tad snug but not too bad.

Liberty's brows shot up as we approached the counter. She elbowed Justice and nodded her head our direction. She leaned toward me. "Did you ask him, Coop?"

"Ask me what?" said Tick.

Liberty directed her attention to him. "Do you know who's in the grave yet?"

Before he could answer, Mama materialized from Lord-knows-where and laid a hand on his shoulder. "Now, what was it you wanted to show me, Keith?" Then she looked over at us. "Y'all three go collect dirty mugs and straighten books, please.

Wipe down tables if necessary. There's no need for five of us to be crammed behind the counter."

Liberty yanked me into the Cookbooks and Crafting aisle. She put her finger to her lips and pointed to where Justice was pretending to straighten an already perfect row of book spines.

It *was* the best spot to eavesdrop on Mama and Tick. Those particular bookshelves were extra wide and had no back to them. Rows of books faced each other, and if you crouched down at the right angle, or stood on a step stool, you could peer over the tops of the books, straight through to the front counter.

"There's a photo I'd like you to take a look at." Tick pulled something—I assumed the photo—from a folder.

Liberty jabbed me. The only thing sharper than her elbows was the pain in my ribs.

"I bet a sack of baseballs that is a picture of whatever the medical examiner guy handed him from out of the grave," she whispered. "Remember how he took a photo?"

"Yeah, but of what?" I said under my breath. "I can't see. Tick is blocking my view."

"Do you recognize this?" Tick held the photo out to Mama. "I've been asking around, but so far, no one seems to know it."

Justice squinted. "What's he showing her?"

I shook my head and elbowed Liberty. "Scoot down. Maybe we can see from a different angle."

She inched over, and Justice and I followed.

"It's beautiful. It looks like a wedding ring."

A wedding ring?

Mama lifted the photo for closer inspection. "Is—is that blood on the band?"

Blood? Now *that* I wanted to see. I stretched high on my tiptoes and peered through the next level of books.

Tick nodded. "I think so. We're getting it tested."

Gramps backed out of the kitchen, carrying two full racks of clean coffee mugs in his strong arms. The door swung back and forth behind him. He set the racks down and started pulling out mugs.

Mama grimaced. "Well, I can't say I recognize it, but we've only lived in Windy Bottom for five years." She turned to Gramps. "Harley, do you recognize this?"

Gramps leaned over her shoulder for a look. He paused.

I jumped at the sound of shattering mugs as shards went flying.

CHAPTER 7

"GRAMPS!" I DASHED DOWN THE aisle and around the corner to his side.

He sagged against Mama.

Tick supported Gramps on his other side and guided him toward a chair. They slowly eased him down. He sank, his face white.

"Gramps?" I crouched at the base of the chair. "You okay? What's wrong?"

Mama moved toward the counter. "I'm calling an ambulance."

Gramps shook his head. "Don't."

She stopped and exchanged a glance with Tick.

He held a hand up. "No. No ambulance."

She scrunched her brow like she was thinking hard. "Harley, I think—"

"How about some water then?" Tick said.

Gramps nodded, and Mama rushed to fill a glass.

"Gramps," I repeated. "What's going on?"

Liberty and Justice stood wide-eyed behind the armchair. In fact, everyone who was in the bookstore circled around Gramps's chair.

Tick squatted down and gently removed his photo from Gramps's grasp. "What is it, Doc? You recognize this ring?"

Gramps took the photo back and traced around the gold ring with his finger. "Tabby's wedding ring."

Gasps filled the room. Mama's hand flew to her chest. Tick slowly stood and locked eyes with Mama.

"Who is Tabby?" Jus whispered to Lib.

"Go get your folks, Justice," Mama said, her voice tight.

"Yes, ma'am." He brushed through the crowd and dashed down the corridor.

Mama turned to Tick. "Let's get Harley back to my office."

Tick nodded. "That's fine." He turned and faced the crowd. "All right, folks, let's give Doc some space."

He helped Gramps to his feet, but then Mama took over and led Gramps through the kitchen to where her office was. I wanted to follow, to let him know it would be all right. But my body was frozen.

Tabby Goodman. My knees felt a little weak. Gramps never

talked about my grandmother. Mama said she'd left Gramps a long time ago, and it was a sore subject. Like that was somehow a perfectly acceptable explanation. But it wasn't. Not to me. I'd always wondered who she was and what she was like, and the fact no one would talk about her felt like I would never know all of who I was.

"Now see here, Vidler." Willy the postman squirmed his way to the front of room. "If that skeleton is Tabby Goodman, then I'm Beyoncé."

"Who's Beyoncé?" croaked a voice from the crowd.

Tick cocked his head. "How you figure, Willy?"

Willy threw his arms up. "Because *everybody* knows Tabby left town forty-odd years ago."

"And y'all saw her leave?" asked Tick.

"No," piped a voice, "but she left a note. And we all saw *that*."

The crowd parted for the Feather sisters and their Friday green-feathered hats.

Miss Ruth looked stricken. "It couldn't be Tabby."

"The big-city girl went back to the big city," said Miss Meriwether.

Heads nodded, followed by a chorus of "that's true" and "I remember."

"See?" Miss Meriwether squared her shoulders smugly.

Mama returned. "Deputy Vidler needs facts, not gossip."

"Fiddle-faddle. Around here they're interchangeable, you know that." Miss Meriwether continued walking to the front and parked herself in front of Tick. Liberty once said that sarcasm was an accessory that Miss Meriwether wore often. And she would know. Liberty was fluent in two languages: Cussing and Sarcasm.

"It's not my place to say, and, mind you, I'm not one for spreading gossip—"

Mama rolled her eyes. "Heaven help me," she whispered.

"—but Tabby's clothes were gone from her closet." She jabbed her finger at Tick. "She wanted to travel. She was a photographer, you know."

"No. I didn't know," Tick said. He looked to the crowd. "So none of you were surprised to hear she'd left town?"

Willy shrugged. "Not really. She tried to fit in, but always was out of place."

"She left a note. Small-town, married life wasn't to her liking." Miss Meriwether drew herself tall and crossed her arms. "I don't care who you *think* is lying in that grave, but whoever is, it sure as heck is *not* Tabitha Goodman."

Miss Ruth nodded her head in sisterly agreement.

"Maybe not," said Tick. "The body hasn't been identified. Just the ring."

Mr. and Mrs. Gordon had joined Mama and Tick at the counter. Liberty, Justice, and I quietly stood next to them.

"We'll watch the store," Mr. Gordon said. "You best take Doc home, Delilah."

I followed Mama and Tick into the kitchen. I wanted to see how Gramps was. But before we got to the office, Tick stopped Mama.

He pulled a black notebook from his shirt pocket and flipped it open. "Do you know who Tabby's dentist was?" He avoided Mama's eyes. "For her old dental records. To establish an ID."

"I never met the woman. Steven didn't even know her. Who was the dentist in town when you two were boys here?"

"Doc Orr—but he retired ages ago. Wonder what he did with his records."

I had an idea and nudged Tick. "What about me? I've seen enough cop shows on TV to know you can use my DNA. If enough of those genetic doohickey things—"

"Genetic markers?"

"Yeah. If enough markers show up on the test, that means the skeleton is my grandma."

Tick glanced at Mama and then at me. "I know this isn't nice news to hear, but it would definitely help get some answers. And, for Doc's sake, we need to make a positive ID as soon as we can."

Mama nodded.

"This is a difficult time, Coop, and I appreciate your

willingness to help. I know your gramps does too. Let me get one of my CSIs down here. We can swab the inside of your mouth and get it to a lab. A cousin of mine teaches at the forensic college in Atlanta. She owes me a favor and should be able to fast-track the results. I still might need to sweeten the deal with a steak dinner, but we should know very soon if the remains are Tabby Goodman's."

CHAPTER 8

WHEN I GOT HOME THAT afternoon from cutting the Feather sisters' grass, Gramps was in his recliner. The *Windy Bottom Breeze*, still folded, rested in his lap as he stared off into space. I guess if you already knew the news, there wasn't much point in reading the paper.

"Hey, Gramps."

He glanced at me as I plopped onto the sofa. There seemed to be more specks of gray in his hair tonight. "Heard what you did for Vidler and getting him some DNA." He sighed. "Thank you."

I nodded. We passed the next several moments in a silence so heavy it felt as though an anvil had been dropped into the room. What do you say to someone whose wife's body may have been discovered? I pushed myself off the sofa. "You don't have any sweet tea, Gramps. I'm going to get you some."

He waved his hand and started to speak, but I dashed toward the kitchen before he could tell me no.

Three different casseroles dropped off by various members of the Windy Bottom Compassion League sat on our counter. Mrs. Alcott had also baked her prizewinning German chocolate cake, and I didn't have to look, but I could smell Earl's formaldehyde-scented muffins. Did he keep his baking supplies in the morgue?

Mrs. Alcott ran the Compassion League, a club of church ladies who cooked food for people when an emergency or illness interrupted normal comings and goings. According to Miss Ruth, it was also a great way to catch up on the local gossip. Usually a spread like what covered our counter required a serious illness or recent death. I reckon the ladies made an exception when Gramps learned that his runaway wife *might* instead have been a murder victim.

Mama shut the refrigerator door and wiped her hands on a dish towel. "How's his headache?"

"I didn't know he had one," I said.

"I'm fine, Delilah," Gramps hollered from his recliner.

She narrowed her eyes like she was trying to decide if he was telling her the truth.

"I don't buy one penny of that statement," Mama said under her breath to me. "Dinner's ready and it will do you good to eat," she called to Gramps.

We had a dining room, but Gramps had turned it into his study ages ago, so we ate at the kitchen table. I liked it better that way. Life was cozier around a kitchen table than some stuffy dining room.

Gramps said grace, but then instead of digging in, spent dinnertime rearranging the food on his plate.

"Harley, eat." I'd never heard Mama use her "don't-argue-with-me" tone on him before.

I could've used my knife to cut the tension instead of the meat loaf.

"What if that really was Tabby lying dead in the ditch?" He glanced up from his plate. "What if she didn't run off?"

Mama peeked at me, then back at Gramps. "Harley, please."

He quit playing with his food and set down his fork. "After she left town, I spent months hoping she'd change her mind and come back to me and Steven. I even set an extra place at the table for dinner each night. Left the porch light on too. Here I was thinking she abandoned us. But what if..." He dropped his head in his hands and sighed. "What have I done?"

"We still don't know for sure the remains *are* Tabby's," Mama said.

He slid his chair back and stood, holding his plate in his hand. He walked over to the trash can, stepped on the pedal to open the lid, scraped the uneaten food into it, and set his plate in the sink. "I'm going for a walk."

Mama set her fork down. "Harley, I don't—"

"I'll be fine, Delilah." Gramps smiled, but it was fake. The smile didn't reach his eyes. "I just want to grab some fresh air. A quick trip around the block. Then I'll be back."

I crammed the last bite of meat loaf into my mouth and quickly swallowed. "I'm finished too, Gramps." I pushed my chair back. "Want me to come with you?"

"Not tonight, son. You'd find me poor company."

My shoulders dropped.

He tousled my hair. "But thanks for the offer." Unanswered questions seemed to cling to Gramps. And something else I couldn't put my finger on. Grief for sure, but something else? Maybe guilt?

No, that was silly. Guilt about what?

"You help with dinner cleanup, Coop," Mama said as Gramps shut the back door behind him. "I'm almost done, and then I'll give you a hand."

Scowling, I picked up my plate and walked over to the sink. I smacked the faucet handle to turn the water on and tried to drown my frustration in dish suds. Gramps's silhouette shrank in the distance as I looked out the kitchen window.

I'd never known much about Tabby. Who was she? Where

did she come from? What did she look like? So many questions. But the question that looped over and over through my mind was, *did she really ever leave Windy Bottom?*

Silence hung in the kitchen air as I washed and Mama dried. We had a dishwasher, but whenever Mama had something pestering her, she'd do dishes by hand. Said drying kept her hands from wringing and her mind from fretting.

"Mama, what do you know about Tabby?"

She sighed but kept drying. "She was your *gran*, Coop. Don't call her Tabby."

I shrugged. "All right, what do you know about Gran?"

"Hardly a thing." She put one plate in the cupboard and picked up another. "I know she was a photographer, and Gramps met her while he was at medical school. They got married, came back here so he could open his practice. She left about a year after your daddy was born."

Poor Gramps.

"Delilah?" Tick's voice sounded down the hall.

"We're in the kitchen, Keith," she called. "Come on through."

"I wanted to swing by and check on Doc." He threw his hat on the table. "Hey, Coop."

"Gramps went for a walk." I said.

"Don't suppose I could talk you into some iced tea while I'm here?" he asked Mama.

"I can do better than that." She waved her hand toward the Compassion League's buffet. "Help yourself."

He rubbed his hands together. "Perfect."

"What did the lab say?" I asked.

"Easy there, Coop." He spun back around to the food on the counter. "Oh, is that Mrs. Alcott's German chocolate cake?"

"Earl brought muffins," I offered.

Tick looked over his shoulder at me, his face twisting. "I'll pass. Thanks."

Mama pulled a chair out and sat next to him as he ate. She absentmindedly rubbed her ring finger. If there weren't dishes to wash to keep worrisome thoughts away, she'd start fiddling with imaginary jewelry that hadn't been on her finger for a couple years.

"Hey, Coop. When I'm done eating, want to play some gin rummy to pass the time until your gramps gets back?" asked Tick.

Tick was a lousy gin rummy player—Texas Hold'em was more up his alley—so I'd no doubt he suggested the game to placate me.

But tonight I needed something that would allow me to stick around maybe longer than they'd want. "How about we build a cardhouse instead?" Cardhouses were quiet. People tend to forget you exist when you're quiet.

The ice cubes from the sweet tea clinked against the glass as he took a sip. "Sure."

"I'll grab a few decks from the living room."

I rummaged through the side-table drawer for cards. The back door opened, and a chair scraped against the floor in the kitchen. Gramps's and Tick's voices carried down the hall as they greeted each other.

I grabbed a deck, slammed the drawer shut, and raced back to the kitchen. Edging my way around the adults, I silently prayed Mama wouldn't banish me from the room. The stool at the breakfast bar offered the perfect out-of-the-way place to eavesdrop unnoticed. I slipped the cards from the box.

Gramps took his glass of water and sat next to Mama.

"Apologies for interrupting your evening, Doc." Tick's hands ran back and forth along the back of the chair in front of him. He faced Gramps. "I got the DNA results back from my cousin." He paused. "I'm sorry to have to tell you, Doc, but it is Tabby."

Gramps dropped his head in his hands. "Sweet Jesus."

"No," Mama whispered.

My insides stiffened.

"I know it's a shock." Tick pulled the chair away from the table and sat facing Gramps. "This afternoon, Meriwether Feather mentioned Tabby had left a goodbye note."

"It's probably a fake, though, right?" I said. So much for me being quiet. "Obviously she didn't run away. Someone killed her and then typed that letter to make it look like she did."

Mama shushed me.

Gramps gazed at the floor. "No. That's just too awful. I can't imagine..." He looked up at Tick. "Is that what you think?"

Tick shifted uncomfortably. "Well... She didn't bury herself." He looked at me. "But that doesn't necessarily mean the note's a fake. She might've been planning on leaving but got interrupted." Tick leaned back in his chair. "I know it's a long shot, Doc, but do you still have that note?"

Gramps took a drink of water. A long one, like he needed time to think, then nodded. "For months I kept it in my pocket. I guess I was hoping if I looked at it enough times I'd see something I hadn't noticed before, and it'd lead me to Tabby. Finally decided to put the note, along with the rest of her things, up in the attic. I couldn't bring myself to throw them away."

He set his glass on the counter. "We can go up there and look."

CHAPTER 9

THE ATTIC SAT AT THE top of a narrow and dimly lit staircase. I'd never explored all its nooks and crannies—just helped Gramps bring down decorations for Thanksgiving and Christmas and such—so I couldn't wait to see what cool stuff was hidden there.

And *seeing* wouldn't be a problem given the fact that after an encounter with a mouse in a box of Christmas decorations a couple years back, Gramps had installed lighting powerful enough to startle any living thing away.

Gramps climbed the stairs first with Tick, Mama, and me following behind. He opened the door and flipped on the light. I waited a couple moments for my eyes to adjust to the brightness. Stuff was scattered willy-nilly. Broken bits and bobs, old furniture, decorations for various holidays, and more.

Tick let out one long whistle.

"I know it looks like a tornado just went through here, but it's actually organized," said Gramps. "I have a system."

"I hope you used a different 'system' to organize your patients' medical files. How can you find anything up here?" asked Mama.

Gramps pointed to the far corner. "Back there is where all her stuff is. I haven't been through it since I hauled things up here."

We started to make our way to a hodgepodge of stacked boxes, old luggage, and trunks.

"Anything you can remember about the note would be helpful," said Tick, stepping over a couple boxes. "Like the kind of paper it was written on and—"

Gramps disappeared briefly behind the fake Christmas tree. "It wasn't handwritten. It was typed. On plain white paper." He reached the corner and picked up one of the boxes from the top of the stack. With a grunt, he handed it to Tick. "Careful. It's heavy." He turned to Mama and me. "How 'bout Keith and I go through the boxes? Delilah, you take those trunks, and Coop, you sift through those bags and suitcases over there?"

"You got it, Gramps." I knelt down and pulled a duffel bag toward me. *I* wanted to be the one to find the note. It would be another way for me to help Gramps besides just giving my DNA.

A musty smell hit me in the face as I unzipped the bag and

pulled the items out one by one. Nothing but shoes and a couple old scarves. Not to be discouraged, I stuffed the items back in, zipped it shut, and pushed it away.

A bulging brown paper sack leaned against a box nearby. I walked over and grabbed it next. Disappointment gnawed at me as I pulled out a pale pink robe and a pair of slippers.

Maybe the suitcase held something more interesting. Gramps had crammed a lot of stuff in it. There were *some* clothes, but mostly it was filled with old magazines. I fanned through the colorful stack. A couple photographs fell to the attic floor. I picked one up. It was of a young guy who looked sort of familiar. I stared at it for a couple moments before I realized it was Gramps—but a *young* Gramps. He held a suitcase in one hand and had his other arm wrapped around a lady wearing an orange-and-white striped dress and a floppy hat. She was almost as tall as he was. They stood on a tarmac, smiling. It must've been taken back in the day when you walked outside to get on a plane.

The lady's orange suitcase was at her feet and something—also bright orange—was slung over her shoulder. I could just make out the letters TG written on the lower left corner of both the bag and suitcase. TG? Tabby Goodman? I'd never seen any pictures of her before.

I held it up to Gramps. "Is this Tab—I mean *Gran*? And what's that thing draped across her?"

Gramps looked up from his box. A smile formed across his face as he nodded. "Yes. That's her. That was taken as we were leaving on our honeymoon." He chuckled. "And that's a camera bag she's got. You don't really see too many of those these days with everyone using phones to take pictures."

"Oh, I'd love to see that, Coop." Mama dropped the armful of dresses she'd pulled from the trunk and waved me over.

I handed her the photo.

"Very pretty." She glanced to Gramps. "She was a classy dresser."

"That was Tabby for you," he said. "Looked like she stepped from the pages of a fashion magazine. Always wore hats outside too. Never did understand women's obsession with hats," he said under his breath.

Mama tapped the photo. "She's wearing a Giovanni Rue design in this picture."

"A what?" said Tick.

Mama pointed to Tabby's dress. "The buttons are the giveaway—they're a Giovanni Rue trademark. Each dress design had its own special style of buttons, and they were always inscribed with his initials. Very expensive."

Tick raised his brow. "How the heck do you know that?"

"I haven't always been a coffee shop owner, now have I? Once upon a time, when I was going to college with no idea of what I wanted to be, I majored in fashion. I just don't gab on about it, that's all."

"How expensive?" Tick asked, gesturing to the photo.

Mama cocked her head. "The label was all the rage, particularly for high-society women. People paid over a thousand dollars back then, and nowadays an authentic Giovanni Rue dress will cost you a month's salary."

"For a dress?" I muttered, walking back to the suitcase. "No wonder Liberty doesn't like them."

Tick turned to Gramps. "Did you buy her that?"

"No. But she had nice clothes. Her folks were well off." He pointed to the photo that had been returned to me. "That dress there was her favorite—she loved the color orange."

That explained the camera bag and suitcase.

Mama gently picked through the clothes in the trunk. "I don't see it here—but these are all gorgeous. Didn't you wonder why she would leave so many expensive clothes behind?"

"I hoped she'd be coming back. She didn't write that she was leaving for good. Just that small-town life was smothering her and she needed to get away."

I picked up the other photo that had dropped from the magazines. It was also of Tabby. She looked so happy. I ran my fingers over the photograph. Daddy got his smile from her. His eyes too. And neither of them were in my life.

A gold chain hung around her neck. I brought the photo closer. A green stone with maybe diamonds surrounding it dangled from a clasp at the bottom. The whole thing was about the size of nickel. I wondered which cost more—an emerald necklace or some dumb dress.

I reloaded all the items except for the two pictures back into the box. I wanted to keep them.

"These clothes are beautiful." Mama pulled a pale-pink dress from the trunk and held it against her body. "She must've looked stunning in this."

Gramps looked up. "That was also one of her favorites. She was a sight." He gazed at the dress as if he could still see her in it. Then he cleared his throat, pushed aside his box, and reached for the next one. "Coop, this box is your dad's," he said reading the words on top. "Looks like it got mixed up with Tabby's stuff."

I jumped and rushed toward Gramps, whacking my leg against an old chair, but I didn't care. Anything that belonged to Daddy was worth a bruised shin. Gramps grunted as he lifted and handed it to me. He frowned at my head. "You need a haircut," he muttered, before turning his attention to another of Tabby's boxes.

It wasn't a big box, but it was heavy. *Steven's Books* was scrawled across the top. I set it on the floor and yanked open the flaps. Hardy Boys mysteries. "Cool," I breathed. Mysteries were my favorite and knowing these belonged to Daddy made them even more awesome. "They're books, Mama."

"Wonderful," she murmured.

I wasn't sure if she meant the discovery of Daddy's books or if she was referring to another dress she'd just pulled from the trunk.

I turned to Gramps. "Can I keep these in my room? Please?"

"Sure," he grunted, digging through more stuff.

I picked up the two photos of Tabby and slid them into the middle of one of the mysteries so they wouldn't wrinkle, then set the box aside to carry downstairs once we were finished.

"Doc," Tick pulled a couple hats out from a trunk and placed them on the ground. "Was there ever an investigation into Tabby's disappearance?"

Gramps threw Tick a dirty look. "I did report her missing. But the police said she was an adult and could leave if she wanted." His fists clenched. "It was so frustrating! Yes, adults can come and go as they please, but I *knew* something was wrong. I *knew* it. And no one would believe me."

Tick nodded. "It's hard to investigate missing persons when they're adults. 'Specially if they packed and left a note saying they were leaving."

"No marriage is perfect, and even if we did have problems," Gramps shifted his weight, "and I'm not saying we did, mind you—but I never thought she'd leave Steven. She loved him so much."

"When the police wouldn't investigate, what did you do?" Tick asked.

"I was frantic to find her. I went to see Ruth Feather. She and Tabby were such good friends. Hoped maybe Tabby had said *something* to her about where she was headed. But Ruth was too shocked and upset to speak. They'd grown so close, you know."

That explained why Miss Ruth seemed so sad at the bookstore when Gramps ID'd the ring.

Gramps continued. "Since the police were being useless, I decided to look for her on my own. I even drove to Atlanta—it's where she was from—and talked to her friends there to see if maybe she had reached out and contacted them. Nobody knew anything.

"I searched for three weeks, but realized I had to get back home to Steven. I was all he had left." He grabbed another box, knelt down, and unfolded the cardboard flaps. "I followed up with the police in Windy Bottom and begged them to search for her. But same old story. They weren't going to look for someone who technically wasn't lost." He rested back on his heels and shrugged. "So I hired a private investigator to keep on looking. After a year, he gave up. Said if she didn't want to be found, she wasn't going to be. And then do you know what he said? Told me to keep an eye on the bank accounts and if there was no movement and no contact made by her for seven years that I could have her declared legally dead." He huffed. "Some investigator."

His face reddened. "I mean, I did think she must be dead, to tell you the truth. I couldn't see her staying away from Steven if she was still alive. But I could never bring myself to have her declared dead." He brushed at his eyes.

Mama's face fell. "Oh, Harley. I'm so sorry. Here I am prattling on about fashion and—and, you're…"

"I'm fine. Really."

"What about her parents?" asked Tick. "Did they search for her?"

"Her parents died before we married. Her father was in the shipping business. But she had her father's lawyer sell the company."

"So she was quite wealthy?" Tick asked.

"She didn't really care much about money," Gramps said. "Didn't ever put on airs. She did like buying expensive clothes, though."

He pointed to the trunk at Mama's feet. "You should have all these. Tabby would want that." He swiped at his eyes. "There! Two good things. You got some fancy dresses," he said to Mama. "And you," he said to me, "got some of your daddy's books." He then glanced at Tick. "I sure don't need Tabby's dresses, but I'd like to keep her necklace. I gave it to her on our first wedding anniversary. That and the ring. Can you get those back for me when you're done processing everything at…the crime scene?" He pulled a hankie from his back pocket.

Tick's brow furrowed. "We didn't find a necklace."

"You must have. She never took it off. *Never.*"

"Can you describe it?" Tick pulled his notebook from his pocket and flipped it open.

Gramps rubbed his face. "It was an emerald surrounded by small diamonds."

I pulled out the Hardy Boys book and looked again. Yep. I snapped a picture with my phone so I'd have a copy, then took the photo to Gramps. "Is this the necklace?"

He looked. "That's it."

"Can I borrow that, Doc?" Tick asked.

"Whatever helps. I know she didn't leave the necklace behind when she left. And if it wasn't in the grave, then where is it?"

"I'll have a couple officers check with local pawnshops to review their records. It's a long shot after all these years, but maybe…"

CHAPTER 10

TICK SCOOTED A BOX ASIDE and grabbed another. "Did Tabby have any enemies, Harley? Anyone ever threaten her?"

Gramps frowned. "*Everyone* liked Tabby. She was kind, funny, generous."

"What about before you moved back to Windy Bottom? Any troubles?"

"We were college students. The most trouble we got into was missing class."

We all fell silent for a bit—three of us digging through boxes and one of us digging through old memories.

"Ah-ha!" Gramps held up a crumpled, yellowed piece of paper. He stood and stepped away from the wooden shoebox-sized box in front of him. "Here it is—in with the stuff from her nightstand."

"Careful," said Tick. He picked a handkerchief from the trunk at his feet and gently took the letter from Gramps. "It may be old, but it's still evidence." He read it out loud.

March 24, 1977
Dear Harley,

I'm not cut out for small-town life. I have to get away. Take care of Steven.

—Tabby

"She certainly kept it short," said Tick.

Mama nodded. "Hmm. It's not very sentimental, is it?"

"I've read medical lab reports with more emotion," said Gramps, with a cough. "I tried to convince the police that she would never have left her son in such a casual manner. But they wouldn't believe me."

"I'm going to run out and grab an evidence bag from my car. I know it's been years, but maybe the lab can pull some prints."

"Fingerprints won't help you none," said Gramps. "Everyone and their hound dog handled that letter after she left. I showed it around when I was looking for her." He coughed again and rubbed his chest. "I must've inhaled some dust up here. I need some water."

We headed back downstairs. Tick set the note on the coffee table and dashed out to his car while Mama walked with Gramps to the kitchen. I pulled my phone out from my back pocket and took a photo of the note. I'd just finished shoving my phone back when Tick reappeared.

Later, up in my room, I opened my laptop, typed "Beethoven" into the search bar, and waited for the music to play. His stuff somehow always helped me think. I took the box of Hardy Boys mysteries off my desk and set them on the floor. I'd go through them later. Right now I had other important things to do. I grabbed a sheet of paper from my desk.

1. Who wrote the goodbye note? Tabby?
2. Where is Tabby's emerald necklace?
3. How did she die?

And most importantly,

4. ✳✳✳Who killed her and why?✳✳✳

The stairs creaked with footsteps. I grabbed a Hardy Boys mystery from the box and laid it open, covering up my questions. Mama was prone to worry, and if she saw my list she might think I was anxious about Tabby's murder.

She walked over to my desk and smiled at the opened book. "Clearly you got your love of mysteries from your dad." Her fingers ran through my hair. "So shaggy." She bent down and kissed the top of my head. "Today was so long I'm thinking both Friday and Saturday happened. Don't stay up too late."

I nodded. "'Night, Mama."

It was only a smidge after nine o'clock, and there was no way I'd be going to bed soon. The day had been so exciting my brain wouldn't be able to shut off for hours. I opened a new tab on my computer and typed "pawn shops" in the search bar. For the next hour, as Beethoven's Fifth blared through my earbuds, I scrolled through, making a list of any pawn shop between Windy Bottom and Atlanta.

I emailed the list to Tick. A couple minutes later, my computer chirped.

Thanks. Also researching when I got your message. You beat me to the punch. Go to bed.

—Tick

CHAPTER 11

THE NEXT MORNING, JUSTICE AND Liberty waited on the top step of my front porch. Mama and Gramps had already left to join the Gordons at A Latté Books. Since the first day of school was Monday, they'd all agreed to let the three of us have this last weekend off.

"Well?" Liberty said, as I opened the front door and let them in.

"Well, what?"

Justice threw his hands up. "Is the skeleton your granny or not?"

"Yes." I jogged back upstairs, leaving them by the door, probably with their mouths open.

"Wait. What? Really?" Liberty caught up to me. "Stop." She grabbed my arm. "Does Tick know how she died?"

"Not yet."

"Is your gramps a suspect?" asked Justice.

I turned around, horrified at the question.

"'Cause, you know," he stopped on the step behind Liberty, "the police *always* think the husband or wife did it."

"Don't be an idiot, Justice," said Liberty. "Doc isn't a suspect."

"Of course not," I said, scowling.

"Where is he, anyway?" she asked. "Taking the day off?"

"Nope. At the bookstore." I passed my room and headed for the attic stairs. "Mama wanted him to stay home, but he said, and I quote, 'the work will keep me distracted.'"

"Where are you going?" asked Liberty, turning her ball cap backward on her head.

"The attic. There are some boxes I didn't get to look through last night. Follow me."

"Boxes?" said Justice.

I told them about looking for the goodbye note and the missing emerald necklace as we climbed the stairs.

"Wow," breathed Liberty. "An emerald and diamonds, huh? Maybe it was a mugging gone bad."

"A mugging? In Windy Bottom? And then, whoever it was, took time to come to the house, write a note, and pack a few clothes?" I shook my head. "Someone in town killed Tabby. I just need to figure out who."

"Yeah," said Justice. "*Before* your grandpa becomes a suspect."

Liberty raised her brow and surveyed the boxes and trunks. "All this stuff was your granny's?"

"Yep." I looked at the mound of boxes. "Maybe there's something here that can help solve her murder."

Liberty shrugged. "Dig in, I guess."

I picked one and Liberty sat cross-legged next to me with a smaller box. Justice walked past us. "I'm going to explore your attic. Then I'll help."

"Y'all ready for school on Monday?" I asked, flipping through old holiday cards.

"Yep," said Liberty.

"Nope," said Justice from behind an old dresser. "Ever since that incident with Silas's goat, Miss Grupe's been out to get me." He puffed out his cheeks. "I tried *telling* her nothing good ever came from reading, but did she listen? No."

Last year, after reading a *National Geographic* article about a mountain goat's ability to leap around steep cliffs, Justice and Silas wanted to see how the goats of Windy Bottom faired in comparison. It was a well-known fact that the highest roof gables in town were on Miss Grupe's house. It took the fire department two hours to corner and remove Silas's goat, Jeffrey, from Miss Grupe's roof. Some of her shingles still hung catawampus. But the general consensus afterward was that a Windy Bottom goat would do just fine on a mountain. So the afternoon hadn't been a total bust.

Liberty huffed. "Just don't do anything stupid this year, and I reckon you'll be fine." She turned to me. "How 'bout you Coop? You ready?"

"Maybe." My box didn't hold anything interesting. Just the holiday cards and some old shampoo bottles. I shoved it aside.

Justice circled around to where Liberty and I sat. He narrowed his eyes. "You worried Beauregard Knapp's gonna be trouble?"

Beau had so many silent letters in his name that I often wondered what they were doing there in first place. And with Beau, it wasn't a case of *if* he'd be trouble, but *when*. It was even rumored that he'd had a *bump* with the law sometime in the past month. We couldn't call it an actual *run-in*, because the report had yet to be substantiated by the Feather sisters.

Liberty spit to the ground below. "Don't worry 'bout Bo Peep. I've got your back."

"I'm not worried about him. We just don't…see eye to eye."

"No one sees eye to eye with Beau," said Justice. "He's the shortest kid in class."

That was because Beau was smarter than a whip and had skipped the fifth grade like a pebble across a pond, landing him in sixth grade with us last year. But brains didn't make him friendly. And the odds that he'd gotten nice over summer were probably about as short as he was.

I pointed to a black garbage bag near the trunk Mama looked through. "Do something useful, Justice. Look in the bag."

"The Knapps have been trouble since the word *go*," Liberty said.

Justice glanced in my direction. "Of course, if Angus Knapp was my daddy, I might have a slant for trouble too. Your gramps knows all about that." He opened the bag. "These are just purses, I think."

A pit viper was friendlier than Angus.

According to the Feather sisters, Angus's wife, Cordelia, contracted a rare form of leukemia and died shortly after Beau was born. Despite the fact Gramps tried everything, Angus never got over the fact she'd died under his care. Angus blamed Gramps. And he passed on his poisonous hatred of Gramps to his son.

"Wait. What is this? It's not a purse." Justice pulled out something orange and unlatched it. "Look, there's a camera in here."

"Hey! Let me see that." I took it from his outstretched hands. "It's Tabby's!"

"How'd you know?" asked Liberty, coming up behind me.

I pointed to the TG on the lower right of the bag. "I recognize this from a photo I have of her and Gramps. I'll show you later." I pulled out the camera.

"Is there any film in it?" asked Liberty.

"I don't know." I flipped it over a couple times. I'd never owned a camera that took film. Was there a door or something?

"Let me at it," said Justice, taking it from my hands. "We used film cameras in yearbook last year. They weren't this old, but at least I know how to check for film." He peered through a small window at the top. A grin spread across his face. "Dude! There's a roll." Seconds later, he slid the film canister into his jean pocket. "I'll take it to school Monday. Mr. Donato will let me use the darkroom."

"Just be careful," I said. "Those are the last photos Tabby ever took. Maybe they're of her and Gramps. Or even baby pictures of Dad!" I grinned as an awesome idea sunk in. "Christmas is a ways off still, but how cool would it be to give Gramps those pictures?"

"Very cool," said Liberty.

"I'll be careful. I promise," said Justice.

That night I pulled out my list of questions and added another. Justice's words had haunted my thoughts for most of the afternoon and evening. I couldn't shake the feeling what he said about police suspecting the spouse might actually…be true.

5. Is Gramps a suspect?

CHAPTER 12

ON MONDAY MORNING, MY ALARM clock shrilled, startling me out of a hard sleep.

The soft thud of a cupboard door closing followed by the clink of coffee mugs meant Mama and Gramps were moving around downstairs. The promise of fresh hot coffee had me shuffling faster toward the kitchen. Mama had let me taste my first sip of joe when I was ten, and I'd been slurping it ever since.

"Morning." I poured myself a cup, added some milk, and dropped in a couple ice cubes to cool it down faster, then joined Gramps and Mama at the table.

Gramps hid behind the opened pages of the *Windy Bottom Breeze*, but managed to grunt a greeting.

"Good morning, yourself. Happy first day of school," Mama

said, layering her toast with a spoonful of strawberry preserves that had been most likely brought over Friday by some well-intended gossipmonger. "Glad you're up. We need to have a family talk."

Gramps folded the paper down. He glanced at the watch. "Bit early for a talk. The sun's barely opened its eyes."

"Harley, you know as well as I do this place breeds gossip faster than bacteria in a dead catfish. We need to be prepared."

"For what?" I took a gulp of coffee.

"For the likes of the Feathers sisters for one. And Suds O'Leary. And Burma. And every other living soul in Windy Bottom." She tapped the table with her finger. "There's going to be gossip flying around until they find out what exactly happened to Tabby. People come crawling out of the woodwork when news like this breaks." She pointed to the newspaper. "I wouldn't be surprised if reporters showed up at the store. You never know."

"As long as they don't show up on our doorstep." Gramps took a long draw from his coffee cup. "What do you suggest?"

She crossed her arms. "It's been three days. By now everyone from here to Atlanta will have heard. You might want to stay home today, Harley. Give yourself time to mourn without the whole town gawking."

She had a point. The sound barrier could be broken from

the speed gossip flew around Windy Bottom—particularly creepy gossip.

"Don't worry about me, Delilah. I'll mourn her when I'm ready. The staring, the talking—both in front of and behind our backs—they're to be expected." He waved his hand in dismissal. "We need to show a united front. I say we just carry on the way we always have."

Mama bit her lip. "So your grand plan is to do nothing?"

"Well," Gramps stroked his chin. "Yes, I guess it is. But that's the point. To show everyone that nothing's changed. Same old, same old."

"Business as usual?" I said, finishing off my coffee.

"I say we just ignore them. Maybe they'll go away," Gramps muttered. "I'm going to get dressed for work."

Mama rolled her eyes. "We don't want them to *go away*. They're our customers."

I stood to take my mug to the sink, but Mama reached across and grabbed my hand. "Coop, the gossiping and such, it isn't only going to be at A Latté Books and around town. It'll be at school. Today's the first day too. Just be aware, okay, sugar?"

"Sure."

She squeezed my hand. "Don't let it get to you."

I could handle it.

Flying alongside the news of the skeleton being Tabby was a rumor that the police had removed the crime scene tape but were still asking questions. And as much as I wanted to see if that was true, the unfortunate fact was the school year had officially ended my summer.

I skidded into Miss Grupe's class five minutes *after* the bell rang. The gray linoleum floor was as ugly as ever. But I loved it, because Gramps had gone to school here and so had Dad. Their memories lived in those scuffs, scrapes, and gouges on the floor.

Miss Grupe was focused on a stack of papers on her desk and hadn't seen me come in late. She might not have even noticed if it hadn't been for Marla-Laine's big mouth. Gramps always said to focus on the positive in people and nobody's perfect, but that was hard when dealing with Marla-Laine. She had about as much positivity as a defunct battery.

"*Shhh*! Everybody, Cooper's here." She whispered it loud enough the classroom next door could've heard. "His grandmother is the you-know-what at the old playground."

Heat rushed to my face. I bet my cheeks matched the color of the red bricks on the outside walls of the school.

"How nice of you to join us today, Mr. Goodman." Miss Grupe looked up from the school forms blanketing her desk and repositioned her glasses. Two tufts of hair near her forehead stuck straight up, making her look like a great horned owl.

"Yes ma'am," I stopped inside the doorway and tried hard not to stare at her head. "My alarm clock tends to get on the lackadaisical side during summer."

"No tardy detentions the first week, Cooper, but please inform your alarm clock that summer is over." She peered over her glasses and smiled.

"Yes ma'am." I shifted my feet. "But it's just Coop, remem—"

Justice ran into my back, shoving me forward. "Sorry, Coop." He faced the great horned owl. "My alarm clock lacks a daisy too, Miss Grupe, ma'am." Then muttered, "Though truthfully, I'm not sure what a flower has to do with—"

Liberty walked in behind him, yanked the dictionary from his pocket, and smacked him on the head with it. "Coop said *lackadaisical*, not *lacks a daisy*."

Justice took it from her hand.

Liberty leaned around his shoulder. "No, no, it's l-a-c-k, not l-a-x."

We'd all had Miss Grupe in sixth grade, so she was already familiar with our shortcomings.

"Ah-ha. Found it." Miss Grupe yanked a piece of paper triumphantly from the pile. She breathed a sigh of relief, then looked at us. "We'll be sure to work on lots of vocabulary for you this year, Justice."

Justice swallowed. "Please don't go out of your way just for me, ma'am."

Miss Grupe chuckled. "It's no trouble at all." She winked.

To say that the relationship between school and Justice was precarious was akin to saying the *Titanic* hit an ice cube.

Lib met Miss Grupe's amused gaze. "I fear vocabulary's gonna be the death of him, Miss Grupe."

She smiled. "Well, we certainly don't need any more deaths. One body in this town is plenty." The smile dropped from her face. "Oh, dear. Coop—I didn't think. I'm sorry." She cleared her throat. "How's your grandfather holding up?"

"It's okay, Miss Grupe. Gramps is fine." I puffed my chest out. "Just business as usual."

"Hmmm. Glad to hear it." She nodded and faced the class. "Recent local events are *not* up for discussion in my class. Are we clear on that, everyone?"

Marla-Laine examined her fingernails.

We made our way to desks near the window.

Justice nudged me. "Mr. Donato gave me permission to use the darkroom tomorrow after school." He dropped his books on his desk. "He's still waiting for some supplies to be delivered."

"Perfect. I'll meet you there." I claimed the desk in front of him. A strategic move. We had learned the year before that it was easier to communicate front to back than side to side. Plus, sitting in the corner front row was safer. Beau Knapp tended to claim the rear of the room as his territory.

We headed to the back to stow away our school supplies.

The classroom—like last year's—was mind-numbingly beige except for Miss Grupe's well-intentioned attempt, which fell flatter than the paint on the walls, to add color by taping posters on any available surface. She even had a poster for the police clothing drive hanging on the far wall.

The back of the room was lined with cabinets and bookshelves. A wall of windows on one side overlooked the playground for the lower grades. Miss Grupe's desk sat up near the front. Dead Fred, the plastic skeleton used for science, hung on his stainless steel stand in the corner, next to the state flag of Georgia and the American flag. As much as I liked school, seeing Dead Fred made me wish the day was done and we were already at the playground checking out the crime scene.

I yanked open the lunch cabinet and tossed my lunch box in.

Ambrose Whiting and Marcus Brown huddled at the bookcases in the back of the room. Ambrose held something in his hand, but I couldn't tell what it was. Knowing those two, it was a toss-up between a bullfrog or a snake. Wildlife was their curiosity; wildlife *in the classroom* was their specialty.

Mackenzie McDaniel organized the Kleenex boxes

by color. If vocabulary were to be the death of Justice, an obsessive-compulsive disorder on color arrangement would be the undoing of Mackenzie. She paused, a maroon box of tissues in hand.

"With the reds or the purples?" Her forehead wrinkled.

"I'd wedge it between the end of the purples, but the beginning of the reds," I said. "It's a good compromise."

She looked up. "Thanks, Coop." She glanced toward the front of the room where Miss Grupe stood talking to Marla-Laine, then leaned toward me. "And I'm sorry to hear about your granny. That's pretty rotten."

I handed her my box of Kleenex, which was an easy navy blue. "Thanks."

"All right, class," Miss Grupe said. "Thank you for putting away your supplies. Take your seats, and we'll begin our first day as seventh graders. Please answer when I call your name." She looked at her attendance list but didn't need to.

Windy Bottom was small enough that kindergarten through eighth grade all met in the same redbrick two-story building. The student population wasn't exactly booming, and there hadn't been a new kid in our class since I'd arrived five years ago.

"Silas Vincent." She glanced up from her list. "How's your goat, Silas?"

"Jeffrey's great. He hasn't eaten anything weird in a while."

His brow scrunched with thought. "Actually, now that I think about it, I *am* missing my umbrella."

A small laugh escaped from Miss Grupe. "Well, hopefully it won't rain until you can locate it. Marcus Browning?"

"Here."

"Marla-Laine Willis?"

"Present," Marla-Laine said. She unfolded her hands and plumped her blond curls. "And may I say you're looking particularly lovely today, Miss Grupe."

"Thank you, Marla-Laine."

"Bootlicker," Liberty muttered.

The Willises were the most prominent family in Windy Bottom, proven by the fact Willis Street was named after them. Their ancestors helped build the town, though the idea that a Willis *ever* participated in manual labor was a hard pill they'd just as soon choke on than swallow.

Miss Grupe continued down the list. "Ambrose Whiting?"

"Here."

Miss Grupe ticked off his name. "Take the bullfrog outside, Ambrose."

"But it's Murphy," he hollered.

"Who's Murphy?" Miss Grupe asked.

He held up the bullfrog. "My brother's pet. He don't know I got Murphy, and if I lose him, he'll cream my corn!"

"He *doesn't* know I *have* Murphy," corrected Marla-Laine.

"You don't got him. He's right here," said Ambrose, clearly confused.

Marla-Laine swiveled around in her chair. "There're tree stumps with IQs higher than yours, Ambrose."

"Don't pick on him," Liberty said, eyeballing Marla-Laine. "Grammar's always had the upper hand with Ambrose. It's like vocabulary is with Justice."

"She's got a point," said Justice.

"Enough!" Miss Grupe rolled her eyes. "Please bring Murphy to me."

"I'd be happy to, Miss Grupe." Ambrose stood. "He just peed in my hand."

Half the room erupted in laughter, while the other half squealed *ewww*.

Miss Grupe sighed and scanned the room. "Put him in that empty shoebox for the day, and Ambrose?"

"Yes, ma'am?"

"No animals tomorrow please."

"Aww." Ambrose plopped Murphy into the shoebox, set the lid on, and put it next to his desk.

"Cooper Goodman."

"Here," I answered. "And it's just Coop, Miss Grupe."

She smiled. "That's right. I forgot."

Miss Grupe almost made it through the rest of roll call before Beauregard Knapp ruined my day by showing up. He'd grown taller over the summer. Maybe the added height had stretched away some meanness.

Miss Grupe arched a brow and watched Beau slump toward the back row.

"Before you settle in, Mr. Knapp, I think I'll have you sit up *front* this year." She punctuated the sentence with a firm smile.

He stopped midway down the aisle and slowly turned. His steely dark eyes scanned the front row. The moment he saw me, his face hardened.

Liberty swore under her breath again as he made his way to the front.

"Hey, Chicken Coop," he sneered, sliding into the empty desk on my right. "I bet ya missed me as much as your granny missed a decent burial."

After school, Liberty, Justice, and I rode our bikes to the abandoned playground to see if rumors about the crime scene tape being taken down were true. If so, the construction crew would be returning to work soon, and then we'd never get a chance to see the gravesite. That wasn't an experience I was willing to pass up.

Some of the construction equipment had been moved, but nothing else had changed since Thursday.

"We'd better be quick." I dropped my bike to the dirt. A torn edge of the bright yellow crime scene tape was caught in the bark of a giant oak tree next to me and flittered in the breeze. "If we're late to the bookstore, you can bet our folks will know we've been here."

"I'm willing to take my time." Liberty kicked a ball of dirt and watched it break apart. "The sooner I show my face, the sooner Mom's going to start blabbing about the Generational Tea. Just the thought of having to wear a dress—a matching dress with Mama at that—is enough to make me want to hurl."

The Generational Tea was a Windy Bottom event steeped in tradition—sort of like the Cow Patty Bingo Plop, but supposedly more refined. Every year, on Labor Day, the Windy Bottom Compassion League sponsored a tea party. Grandmas, mothers, and daughters would dress the same, sip tea, and eat cookies. Or at least that's what Justice and I had been told. Given the fact we weren't girls, we'd never been invited. Given the fact Liberty had to wear a dress, she *wished* she had never been invited.

"Forget dresses. Let's look where the skeleton was." Justice grabbed Liberty's arm and dragged her with him. "I want to see if there's any bones left."

We walked over and stared silently into the grave that had

kept Gran's body a secret for so many years. Shriveled roots and twigs poked through the clay sides. They looked like nightcrawlers who'd wiggled halfway through, got tuckered out and quit, and then dried up in the hot Georgia sun.

But that was it.

No bones.

No torn piece of fabric from the dress she was found wearing.

No jewelry.

Not even a solitary tooth.

Nothing to show Gran had lain there until she was no more than a bony frame.

CHAPTER 13

TUESDAY MORNING LIB, JUS, AND I crossed Willis Street and walked into the schoolyard.

"Aw, crud." Justice rubbed his forehead. "We had homework, didn't we?"

"What do you think Coop and I were working on yesterday? We had five math questions. And it's a little late to be asking about homework, don't you think?" Liberty scowled.

"Why can't Miss Grupe ease us into homework like a normal teacher? I'm going to head to the library and do it real quick." He took off.

Liberty glanced at her watch.

"I'm going to the library too. I told Mrs. Garcia I'd be her aide this year."

"See ya." I hoisted my backpack onto my shoulders and headed for Miss Grupe's class.

Had I known Beau would be the only other kid in the room when I walked in, I would've joined Liberty and Justice in the library. He sat at his desk.

"Hey, Chicken Coop." His lips curled. "Your grandpa locked up yet? I bet the police will get him for murder *this* time."

I slammed my books on the desk and glared. "What did you say?"

He stayed in his seat. "You heard me."

I took a step toward him. "What's wrong, Bo Peep? Scared to repeat it?"

He slid from his chair. "Scared of you? Not likely."

We stood inches apart, glowering.

Miss Grupe walked into the room carrying a tower of history books. She peeked around the stack. "Ah, good. Helpers. You two can pass these out for me."

I glared at Beau before taking an armload of books from Miss Grupe. I imagined each desktop was Beau's face as I dropped a book onto it.

Within moments, the bell rang, and the hallway filled with the sounds of footsteps, voices, and lockers opening and shutting.

Justice walked in and slid into the seat behind me. "Finished just in time."

Liberty nearly plowed over Miss Grupe, who now stood in the doorway talking with Mrs. Riddle from next door.

"Sorry, Miss Grupe!"

Liberty gripped her ever-present baseball in her hand and motioned to Justice and me as she slid into her seat. She did a double take at me. "Who filled *your* boots up with manure?"

"Beau's just being a jerk." I sat in my seat. "What's up?"

The ball arced over her head and she caught it without even looking. "Guess what I overheard Leroy telling Mrs. Garcia?"

Leroy was the janitor, and aside from his dislike of being called *Mister Leroy*, his claim to fame was being related to Earl. The funeral parlor owner and Leroy were cousins—twice removed on Earl's mother's side according to town gossip.

She tossed the ball the opposite direction and blindly caught it again.

I propped my elbows on my desk. "What?"

"Leroy said the police had been around asking questions."

"Why?" I asked.

She poked Justice. "Remember that whole fiasco involving Rutherford Willis's 'long-lost uncle' a few years back?" Into the air once more the ball flew.

Justice nodded. "It satiated the Feather sisters' need for gossip for quite a while."

The baseball fell to the floor. Liberty *never* dropped a ball.

"*Satiated*." She whistled low. "Wow, Justice. And you used it correctly too."

"I learnt it yesterday." He interlaced his fingers and stretched his arms forward proudly.

"Learned," Liberty and I muttered together.

"Can we get back to the police asking questions and the 'long-lost uncle' bit?" I said. "I've never heard *this* story before."

"Yeah, yeah." Liberty bent down to pick up the ball and then looked toward the door, probably to make sure Miss Grupe and Mrs. Riddle were still talking.

Beau hung out in the back of the room, which was good. The last thing I wanted was him listening to anything involving Tabby.

"Long time ago some guy waltzed into town claiming to be Mr. Rutherford Willis's long-lost uncle."

Justice took over. "Mr. Willis refused to share any of the family fortune until the guy proved he really was a blood relative."

"How'd he do that?" I asked.

"This is the good part." Liberty paused. "They dug up old Mr. D."

My eyes widened. "Really? Why not just do a blood test or something?"

Lib shrugged. "Beats me. Rumor had it Mr. Willis refused to help 'the charlatan'—that's what he called him. But when they exhumed old Mr. D's body, the family noticed the gold ring he was *supposed* to have been buried with was missing!"

"Grave robbers?"

Justice shook his head. "Nope. Earl."

"Earl?" I repeated.

Liberty nodded. "Yeah. When questioned about it, Earl babbled on about how he'd *thought* the ring was on Mr. D's pudgy finger when the coffin closed, but after the burial he noticed it still sitting on the mortuary counter. He was ashamed about the mistake and said he intended on returning the ring once a 'sufficient period of mourning' had passed, but forgot."

Miss Grupe laughed loudly at something Mrs. Riddle said. Thank goodness the bell hadn't rung yet. I wanted Liberty to finish her story.

I scooted to the edge of my seat. "Did they believe Earl?"

"Don't know. But he scurried to the safe and gave them the ring. It seemed like a harmless mistake at the time, but a few months later when Miss Tilda died—"

"Of boredom," Justice interrupted.

"She was the librarian before you moved here," Liberty explained. "And she didn't die of boredom. She was eighty-two and had a stroke."

I nodded. "Get to the point."

"The *point* is her diamond brooch disappeared hours before her service. Her relatives called the police."

My eyes widened. "Whoa. An investigation?"

She nodded. "Turned out Earl had already spent time in the slammer—twice! For stealing off the dearly departed. Guess he reckoned if they'd gone on to receive their heavenly treasures they wouldn't be needing their earthly ones."

Justice nudged my back. "But Earl found the brooch *right* before the funeral."

"Yeah," huffed Liberty. She used finger-quotes. "'Found' it. And Chester's sterling silver dog tag Aunt Leslie sent when we first got him wasn't on his collar after Earl tried to bury him. He said it was missing when he found Chester, but…" Liberty voice trailed off.

"You think he stole it?" I asked.

"Yeah, I think he stole it."

"So why are the police talking to Leroy?" I asked. "Why not Earl?"

"Because," Liberty said, "Earl's made himself scarce."

I inhaled sharply. "You mean he's gone missing?" I remembered how the sign on his door read CLOSED yesterday. He'd skipped town? *Is Earl the murderer? Had he stolen Tabby's necklace?*

"Maybe he accidently got himself locked in a coffin again," muttered Justice.

Just then, the bell rang, and Miss Grupe waved goodbye to Mrs. Riddle.

"There's more—and you're going to freak out over this."

Liberty crooked her finger and motioned me to lean in. "Leroy told Mrs. Garcia that the police told him the blood on your *grandma's* ring…is Earl's."

My jaw dropped. "Why would Earl's blood be on her ring?"

Liberty locked eyes with me. "That's what the police want to know too."

CHAPTER 14

AFTER LUNCH, MISS GRUPE WAITED at the top of the stairs for those of us who needed to put our lunch boxes away in the classroom before heading down to the library. Ambrose and Marcus were staring at Dead Fred and dropped their voices to a whisper when I walked in.

"Uh, Coop?" Ambrose shifted back and forth on his feet.

"Yeah?"

He pointed to Dead Fred behind me.

I turned. Dead Fred's hand was raised in greeting, and he had a name tag stuck to his bony clavicle. It read *Hello, My Name is Tabby Goodman*.

Gran.

My gran.

I stiffened like a stone statue. My breath caught in my throat, but I managed to walk over and rip off the name tag.

"We didn't do it, Coop," Marcus said, walking up to me. "I—I promise."

I breathed in deep through my nose. "I know you didn't."

Ambrose joined us. "Someone must have stuck it on there during lunch when the room was empty."

I nodded. "I've got a pretty good idea who that *someone* was."

I wanted to run to Miss Grupe and show her the name tag. I wanted her to punish Beau. But more than anything, I wanted to give Beau what he deserved. Daddy would've handled it on his own, not run off and tattled.

"Marcus, Ambrose, and Coop." Miss Grupe's voice called from down the hall. "We're waiting."

Marcus dropped his hand on my shoulder. "Come on, man. Let's go."

We got to the library, and Beau shoved his hands in his pockets and slouched over to the graphic novels. Warning bells sounded in my head. *Leave it alone*, they rang.

I went after him anyway.

Justice pulled me back. "Dude. Where you headed? Help me find a book."

I shook his arm loose. "Just give me a sec."

I quickly closed the distance between Beau and me and stood next to him. "You wrote the name tag, didn't you?"

He looked up from the book he held. "What if I did? Everyone knows your granny's the one in the grave. It happened a long time ago, so get over it. It was funny."

"Funny?" Heat rose up my neck. "You think it's funny?"

"Hysterical." He smirked. "And you want to know something else?"

"No." My hands curled into fists.

"Your granddad probably put her there and just *told* people she ran off. Everyone's thinking it." Beau leaned in toward me. "I'm just the one saying it."

My fist slammed into his nose.

Beau's book went sailing, and his feet flew out from under him. I didn't wait for him to hit the floor. I attacked with the ferocity of a rabid raccoon, my fists pummeling into his sides.

Beau tried to shove me off. "My nose!" he howled. "You broke my nose!"

He managed to land a hard punch to my eye. It felt like his whole fist went through my head. Bookshelves and people's faces blurred around me. My eye vibrated with pain, but I kept hitting.

"Cooper Goodman!" Miss Grupe's voice rang through my ears. "Stop now!" She yanked me off Beau and shoved me into a chair. "Don't move," she said through clenched teeth.

Mrs. Garcia arrived with a handful of tissues. Beau sat up and grabbed them from her hand.

"Hold your head up, Beau, and pinch," Miss Grupe instructed, leaning down to look at his face. "It will help stop the bleeding."

Mrs. Garcia hurried toward her office. "I'll grab more tissues," she said over her shoulder.

Beau glowered. Without a doubt, I was on his menu. My classmates circled around us, not daring to say a word except for Liberty and Justice. That's because she was curious, and he was just oblivious as to when to keep his mouth shut.

"What happened, Coop?" Liberty asked.

"Yeah," said Justice. "This is the most excitement *I've* ever had in the library."

"Justice!" Miss Grupe stood. "Fighting isn't excitement. It's disgraceful." She turned to me. "I never expected this kind of behavior from a Goodman." She shook her head, walked over to the library desk, and picked up the phone. I heard the words "Principal Bartberger," "Cooper Goodman," and "fight."

Mama and Gramps would be angrier than hornets in a soda can. I sagged in the chair. My hand hurt from punching Beau. My eye throbbed. There was blood on my shirt, but it wasn't my own. That made me feel a little better, though I knew it shouldn't have.

Beau stopped staring at the ceiling and turned his face to

me. His beady eyes became narrow slits. "You still go to church, Chicken Coop?"

"Yeah," I muttered. "So?"

"So you'd better give your heart to Jesus 'cause your butt is mine." He took away the tissues. "By the time I'm done with you, you'll wish you were in that dirt hole with your granny."

CHAPTER 15

"WHAT IN BLUE BLAZES WERE you thinking?" Mama's words sliced through the air like a thrown dagger. Both she and Gramps had left the bookstore to meet with Principal Bartberger before bringing me home to serve my two-day suspension sentence.

She hadn't breathed a word in the car she was so angry, but now that we were home, her vocabulary was coming on strong.

She threw her keys onto the kitchen table. "Well, Coop?" Both hands rested on her hips. "Let's hear it."

"I was—"

"I don't want to hear it!"

"But you just—"

"Don't argue with me, Cooper Steven Goodman." She marched down the hall into the living room.

I glanced at Gramps. He always took my side in an argument. He'd understand why I had to fight Beau. But instead he crossed his arms and stood silent. I swallowed the lump of disappointment and followed Mama.

"Absolutely unbelievable." She paced in front of the fireplace. "As if we didn't have enough on our plates as it is."

I knew that last remark was about Gran. Even though Gramps had tried to act like life was "business as usual," I could tell he was a train wreck inside. Mama had put on a happy face for both of their sakes.

"I was defending the family honor!" I almost stomped my foot but stopped just in time. I clenched my fists instead.

"Honor?" Gramps walked over to the recliner and sank into the chair. "Where's the honor in starting a fight?"

I straightened and faced Gramps. "I didn't start it." Sure, I threw the first punch, but Beau accused Gramps of killing Gran and dumping her body in that hole. I was being a man and standing up to him. "And there *is* honor in fighting. Daddy fought." I turned and jabbed my finger at the glass box that held Daddy's flag.

"Cooper Steven Goodman, that's enough!" Mama's eyes simmered with a mixture of anger and disappointment. "You will not talk to your grandfather that way."

Gramps sighed and stared at the floor before looking up

at me. "Coop." His voice was a total contrast to Mama's outrage. "Your father fought to help others, not to help himself."

Mama rubbed her temples. "The fact that you would beat up Beau Knapp is unthinkable! The poor kid has so little going for him in life as it is, and you go and pull a stunt like this."

She grabbed her keys from where she had dropped them on the kitchen table. "And on top of everything, the delivery truck is due at the coffee shop any minute. We can't stay and babysit you."

"I don't need a babysitter!"

"You sure?" Gramps stood. His voice was low and soft. "Because your actions this morning proved otherwise."

I winced.

Mama nodded. "We're going back to the store. You will stay here. There will be no television or anything electronic. You will clean the entire house and do all the laundry. Once you finish, read a book or start on the schoolwork Miss Grupe gave you." She jabbed her purse under her arm. "And you will not leave. Understand?"

I slouched against the wall. "Yes, ma'am."

"And if there's something in your laundry that doesn't fit anymore, wash it, and set it aside for the police clothing drive," she added.

I trudged upstairs to my room after she and Gramps left and flung my backpack across the floor. To make life worse, now

I couldn't meet Justice and Liberty in the darkroom to develop the photos from Gran's camera. I flopped on my bed and stared at the ceiling. Beau was lower than a snake's belly. He got what was coming to him. The whole idea of Gramps being responsible for Gran's death and then burying her was stupider than the look on Beau's face right before I punched him.

I sat up and stared at my reflection in the mirror. My eye wasn't swollen shut yet, but it was turning an ugly shade of purple. A few drops of Beau's blood had stained my shirt. Well, good. I peeled it off and tossed it into my laundry hamper in my closet, and caught sight of the box of Dad's Hardy Boys mysteries I'd shoved there Saturday night.

That's what I'd do—go through Dad's box. Mama told me to read, and it didn't matter I'd already read every Hardy Boys mystery back in fourth grade. Rereading them would be like spending time with Dad. Touching something he'd held was as close as I would ever get to feeling him again. And I bet he would've understood why I punched Beau.

Of course, I'd have to clean the house and do the laundry first. Mama would tan my hide if she and Gramps came home and found those things not done.

I might have just gotten myself suspended from school, but I wasn't dumb.

In between laundry loads I vacuumed, dusted, and wiped down every surface that had the potential to reflect Mama's irritated face if she found it not done to her standards. It was three hours of my life I'd never get back, but at least I could spend the rest of the afternoon reading since I'd finished all my chores. I just had to wait for the final load of Gramps's laundry to finish drying. He had a ton of shirts—most dotted with coffee stains. I wondered if he'd notice if I donated a few to the clothing drive.

Before dragging the box of Dad's books from the closet, I added a new question to my list.

6. Where is Earl? Did he steal the emerald necklace?

Then I grabbed the books. Reaching in, I pulled out two or three at a time, then spread them out on the floor. Then I did it again. And again. I kept doing it until the box was empty. The last group of books felt fatter in my hand. I set them down and found layered between two mysteries was a different book.

I brushed the dark brown leather cover. It was soft, and the edges of the paper were gold—like in Mama's Bible. Only it wasn't a Bible. It was a journal. Maybe Dad's from when he was a kid?

I flipped open the inside cover.

Tabitha Goodman.

No, wait—it was Gran's!

Gramps had said Dad used to look through her things in the attic. Maybe he found the journal and kept it with his books. And now I had it.

"Thanks, Dad," I said quietly.

Maybe there was something in her journal that could tell me why she was murdered. The Hardy Boys could wait. I had a *real* mystery and maybe just got my first *real* clue. I climbed onto my bed and leaned back against my pillow. What secrets did Gran's journal hold? Did she write about just herself? Or did she add in some things about Gramps? She might've even written about Dad. My stomach tightened with anticipation as I opened to her first entry.

I tossed Gramps's clean socks into his dresser drawer but it wouldn't fully close. I groaned. I wanted to get back upstairs to Gran's journal. So far it was pretty mind-numbing stuff like what she cooked for dinner or her struggles to make friends— although she did write Miss Ruth was fun. She hoped they'd be good friends. Oh, and how the construction of the new Piggly Wiggly had stirred up a rat colony. Rats and dinner were about as exciting as it got, but I was holding out hope things would get interesting soon.

I shoved against the bottom drawer. Paper crinkled. I squatted, pulled the drawer from the dresser, and peered into the space. Crumpled papers sat wedged in the back of Gramps's dresser. I pulled them out, and torn bits of a photograph fluttered to the ground.

Why would Gramps keep a torn-up photo?

I shook all the photo pieces loose and flattened out the other papers—just a couple of old receipts, one for a cheeseburger and one from Suds' Windy Bottom Gas and Bait.

Someone had worked really hard to obliterate the image of the photo—the pieces were tiny. A long time later, I sat back on my heels and stared at a wedding photograph. It was the size that would fit into a wallet. It was of Gramps and Tabby. She held a bouquet of flowers, and he wore the ugliest pale blue tuxedo I'd ever seen. But despite Gramps's questionable wardrobe choice, they were smiling.

Something must have brought out the bear in him to rip their wedding photo to smithereens. But still he just couldn't bring himself to trash the last shreds of a memory.

I let out a long breath. One of the shreds flipped over. Was that a smudge of ink on the back? I turned over more pieces. Something had been scrawled across the back of the photograph. As I flipped more pieces, the message, with some of the letters blurred, slowly appeared.

I'm sorry
Never Again

Hairs lifted on the back on my neck. Gramps didn't have to sign it in order for me to recognize his sloppy doctor handwriting. What did he mean? What had he done that he would never do again? Was it something awful? Why would he write such an alarming note on a photograph...and a wedding one at that?

CHAPTER 16

A CAR DOOR SLAMMED. VOICES traveled in from outside: Mama and Gramps. I quickly scooped up the pieces of the picture and stashed them in my pocket. I'd tape it together later.

The back door opened. Footsteps moved through the kitchen. Keys dropped on the kitchen table.

"Cooper?" Mama called.

Cooper. Yep. She was still mad.

"Cooper? Where are you?"

I shoved the drawer back into the dresser. "Coming, Mama." I walked out of Gramps's room. "I was putting laundry away."

She nodded. "You can help Gramps get dinner ready. He said he'd cook tonight."

"Yes, ma'am."

She gripped the banister and began to drag herself upstairs but stopped and turned around. "Cooper, about this morning." She took a step down. "What happened? I'll listen now."

I raised a brow.

A hint of a smile appeared. "I promise."

I sat on the bottom stair and she joined me.

"Beau was badmouthing Gramps," I murmured, not wanting Gramps to overhear me from the kitchen. "Called him a murderer and a liar." And then I told her about the name tag on Dead Fred.

"Yeah." Mama kept her voice low and calm. "That *would* be upsetting. But, Coop, it doesn't matter what other people say, because *you* know the truth. You're going to hear things all your life that might make you mad, and you can't react with a punch every time." She held her hands out and then clenched them. "Did you know your brain is almost the same size as your two fists put together? Know what that means?"

I thought of saying it meant I should fight twice as often as I think, but settled for the safer answer. "No."

"It takes *two* fists to equal *one* brain. I'm not saying don't ever react, but I am saying *think* about your reaction good and hard. Violence is rarely the answer." She cocked a brow at me. "You can't shake someone's hand if it's curled into a fist. Understand?"

"Yes, ma'am."

"Good." She stood and went upstairs. "See you at dinner."

I joined Gramps in the kitchen. Maybe I could figure out a way to ask him about the torn photo. Lord only knew how though. He'd already arranged slices of zucchini on the broiling pan. "We'll roast these along with some salmon. Your mama likes fish, and she could use a little pampering tonight, don't you think?" His voice was tight.

The stink of salmon assaulted my nose, but I'd eat crow if it meant being back in Mama and Gramps's good graces.

"Yes, sir."

"Crack that back window open, would you? There's a reason they don't make salmon-scented candles."

A crack wasn't going to cut it. I opened the window all the way. And decided to ease in with a question for Gramps. "So, I was thinking about stuff while you were gone."

"Hmmm?" He concentrated on drizzling olive oil over the zucchini.

"Oh, you know," I shrugged. "Like how sometimes we do things we regret when we're angry."

Gramps nodded. "You regretting that fight with Beau? I hope so. That'd show some maturity on your part."

I *did not* regret my fight with that low-lying snake, but I wasn't about to argue the point.

I cleared my throat. "So...umm...have *you* ever done anything you've regretted, Gramps?"

He grunted. "Of course. There's only ever been one perfect man to walk this earth, Coop, and it's sure not me. Hand me the salt."

I sighed. This wasn't working. "But what about when you get angry? I mean *real* angry. Give me an example. And…and it doesn't have to be a recent time. It—it could've been from years ago. Have you ever…you know…done something?"

"Like punching someone?" He got a funny, faraway look in his eyes. "Nope. I'm not the violent type. I learned a long time ago it's best to settle things quiet-like. And," he looked at me almost coldly, "I'd take whatever steps necessary to make sure that I'd never again have the same problem with that person."

I gritted my teeth. "Okay, so maybe not *punching* someone, but have you ever, say, like…destroyed something?"

Gramps wrinkled his forehead. "What are you playing at? Are you saying, in some convoluted way, that you have anger issues? Did you punch a wall or something?"

He looked around him, maybe searching for holes in the Sheetrock. This conversation wasn't heading in the direction I was trying to steer it.

"No, Gramps!" I rolled my eyes. "Sheesh. I'm just curious. I—"

Someone knocked on the front door.

"I'll get it," I said, welcoming the chance to step away.

Tick stood at the door. Behind him was another deputy—tall

and built like a grizzly bear. I swallowed and gestured for them to come in.

"Hey, Coop." Tick fidgeted with the brim of his hat. "Your gramps home?"

"In the kitchen," I said.

He sniffed the air and walked toward the kitchen. "Fish?"

The grizzly bear removed his hat and followed Tick.

"Yep."

"'Evening, Vidler," said Gramps, his head practically in the oven. He did a double take at the sight of the other deputy.

"This is Deputy Gomez." Tick gestured with his head.

Gramps nodded a greeting. "Have a seat. Salmon should be out in about ten minutes if you want to stay for dinner."

Both remained standing.

Tick rested his hat on the table. "I'm afraid it's not a social call, Doc." He rubbed the back of his neck. "We're here on official business."

Gramps pulled out a chair and looked my direction. "Coop, go tell your mama that we've got company."

Tick waved his hand. "Oh, don't bother Delilah. It's you I came to see, Doc."

"Don't bother who?" Mama brushed past me. "Hello, Keith." She ran her fingers up the side of his arm as she passed.

Tick stiffened.

She faced the man with Tick. "And you are…?"

He shifted his hat under his other arm and reached out his hand. "Deputy Gomez, ma'am."

She furrowed her brow and sat next to Gramps. "What's up?"

Tick met Mama's eyes. He looked to me and darted a glance back to Mama.

She swiveled in her chair to me. "Coop. You're grounded, remember? Up to your room."

She couldn't be serious! Not now. "But, but…dinner—"

"I'll bring you up a plate." She pointed to the doorway. "Go on."

I knew when my bacon was burned, but I also knew where to find another hog. Even though I was grounded and might get more consequences, there was *no way* I was going to miss out on what Tick or Deputy Gomez had to say. Not when there was a perfectly good oak tree right outside my bedroom window. I scurried upstairs to my room, climbed out my window, and shimmied down the tree before dashing around to the backyard.

"…cause of death was acute arsenic poisoning," Tick was saying as I hunkered down under the kitchen window.

A chair scraped against the floor. Footsteps shuffled across the wooden planks. A cupboard was opened and closed. Water poured from the tap of the kitchen sink into a glass.

Tick cleared his throat. "Doc, because of the…uh…circumstances surrounding Tabby's murder—"

"Circumstances?" Mama cut in sharp.

A mosquito wailed near my ear. I shooed it away.

"Doc, were there marital problems?" Tick sounded like he wanted to melt into a puddle. "Fights? Money issues?"

"What? How dare—no! No—of course not. You talked to Earl, didn't you? What has he been telling you?"

"The district attorney considers you a person of interest. A record search showed you bought arsenic three weeks before your wife died," Deputy Gomez said.

"For heaven's sake!" Gramps shouted. "I was a doctor. For years, arsenic, in a highly diluted form, has been used to treat various ailments."

"But you're the one with the motive," Deputy Gomez said. "You stood to benefit the most from her death. Financially."

I wondered if Gramps's face was red. Or if the vein in his neck that always twitched when he got mad had got to twitchin' yet. And what did Gomez mean by saying Gramps would benefit financially? Gramps had been the town doctor. He wouldn't have been hurting for money.

Sheesh. Just because Gran had some money to her name when she died hardly gave Gramps a strong motive to kill her.

Mama's voice quaked. "This is ridiculous! What are you saying? Harley wouldn't hurt a fly!"

Tick let out a strained sigh. "Delilah—"

A chair skidded across the floor and hit the wall.

"Don't you *Delilah* me, Keith Vidler."

"Delilah, please." Tick's tone grew soft, like he was using his voice to defuse a bomb set to explode...that bomb being Mama. "He needs to come in for questioning."

"Now hold on." A hand pounded the countertop. "I did *not* kill my wife!"

I was pretty sure Gramps's family tree could be traced back to Honest Abe. If he said he didn't kill anybody, he didn't kill anybody.

"Are you nuts?" Mama said.

"You're not arresting Gramps!" I shouted through the window.

The four of them were still staring at the kitchen window when I busted through the back door.

"Cooper!" Mama said. "What—"

I marched over to Tick. "You were supposed to help him, not throw him in a cell!"

Tick put his hands up. "I'm not throwing—"

Deputy Gomez took a step toward me. "He's not arresting him, son—"

"I'm *not* your son." Then I turned and glared at Tick. "And I'm not yours, either. My dad is dead." I clapped my hands over my mouth. Because what I should've said: *Gramps is my dad...sort of.*

Tick nodded.

Deputy Gomez rested his thumbs on his utility belt. "It isn't a request. He needs to come with us to answer some questions."

Gramps stood. "Don't worry, Coop. We'll get this straightened out. I'll go with Keith and answer his questions. This is just a formality, right, Keith? Why, I've known you since you were in diapers. You know I didn't kill my wife."

Tick sagged as though standing was a struggle for him. "That brings me to my next point." He paused before continuing, like he didn't want to have to say what was coming next. "I'm no longer working this case. I can't. Because of my relationship with you. The chief decided it'd be best if someone else took over. The county temporarily assigned Deputy Gomez." His hands dropped to his side. "I'm here more as…a…friend."

Tick sounded pathetic.

Gramps scoffed.

Mama stared in disbelief.

"Some friend," I muttered.

"This isn't what I wanted," Tick continued. "You have to understand that." He looked at Gramps. "This particular district attorney—he's young. It's an election year and he's trying to make his record shiny."

Mama gave a stone-faced nod, but said nothing.

"Dr. Goodman," Deputy Gomez said. "We need to search the house. I've got officers waiting outside."

"What the devil for?" Gramps turned to Tick. "We already searched her things. *You* were there."

Tick held his hands up. "I know, but—"

"I can come back with a warrant if necessary," Deputy Gomez said.

The way he treated Gramps was really beginning to tick me off.

The vein on Gramps's neck had gone from twitching to pulsating. "Search the whole house for all I care." He crossed his arms.

Gomez turned to Gramps and gestured toward the door. "Dr. Goodman, if you don't mind, let's head to the station while the officers are engaged here."

Gramps looked to Mama. "Call my lawyer. Vernon's number is in my office—above my desk. Have him meet me at the police station."

She nodded.

I hugged him.

He wrapped his arms around me and held tight for several moments. Then Tick walked outside with him toward Gomez's squad car and opened the car door for him. Gramps waved to me as he was driven away.

Three policemen I didn't recognize stood next to their cruisers. Tick gestured for them to come inside.

They were going to search the house and try to find something to make Gramps look guilty. I didn't know them, and I already didn't like them, and I especially hated Tick. "Traitor," I said under my breath.

Then a realization hit me: If they found Gran's journal, they would take it for sure. I wasn't finished reading it. Thank goodness the wedding photo from Gramps's dresser was still in pieces in my pocket. They'd think Gramps was guilty for sure with that creepy message on the back. A sour taste formed in my mouth. I had to keep them out of my room until I could hide the journal. I needed time, which meant I probably needed to act nice.

"Umm," I turned to the officers. "How about I show you guys to the attic? That's where her stuff is."

"I got it, Coop," said Tick, "but thanks. Watkins, you come with me. Harrison, take the second floor, and Caesar, you can start here. Coop, you and your mama need to stay downstairs, please."

"But, but—wait!" I yanked on Tick's arm.

He stopped and raised a brow. The other two paused at the base of the stairs.

"Uh, umm. My homework. Can I at least get that from my room?" I leaned toward Tick. I pointed to my black eye. "You might've heard already, but I was in a bit of a brawl with Beau Knapp today."

Tick nodded.

"I'll be spending the next couple days at home," I said. "Miss Grupe gave me a ton of work. I need to get started right away… It's for my own safety."

"Your own safety?" asked Tick.

"Mama's madder than a bull with his horns caught between fence rails," I whispered with a shrug.

Tick gave me a small smile. "Move fast and only grab your homework. Nothing leaves the house, and I check your backpack."

"Yes, sir." I dashed upstairs, their footsteps falling behind my own. I didn't have much time. I jammed the journal into the back of my jeans and pulled my shirt down. A quick check in the mirror proved nothing was showing. I slung my backpack across my shoulders and nearly collided with Tick outside my door.

"Whoa, Coop. Let's check the bag."

I spun around so the backpack faced him. He unzipped it and looked around. "Books and lots of work to be done." He zipped it up. "Get going."

"I've got more reading now than I ever even knew existed," I said over my shoulder. Once downstairs, I slipped the journal from my waistband into my backpack to read later.

Watkins and Harrison headed for their cruisers; each with a couple boxes in their arms. Officer Caesar followed behind with a typewriter. I didn't know what was inside the boxes but only that they'd spent a ton of time in Gramps's study, after searching the attic and second floor.

I whirled around and faced Tick. "Why did they take his typewriter? Do they think it's the typewriter the note was typed on? If Tabby typed it, of course it was. Duh! Gramps isn't the murderer."

"No one's saying he is, Coop," said Tick. "They're analyzing the letter your grandmother left. The paper, the ink—anything that might lead us to *who* typed it."

"Even if it was typed on that typewriter, I bet it wasn't by Harley," Mama said. "You know how things are around here. No one locks their doors *now*, let alone back then. Anyone could've used that typewriter."

Mama squeezed my shoulder as we stood on the porch, watching them drive away.

"It'll be okay, Coop," she said. "You'll see." She ignored Tick, who stood a couple feet back.

Her words fell to the ground, empty and lifeless. I didn't *know* if it was going to be okay.

CHAPTER 17

I COULDN'T SLEEP. I THREW off my covers, sat up, and leaned against the headboard. The digital numbers on my clock rearranged themselves: 11:47 p.m. Moonlight flooded through the window and clung to the walls. I hadn't bothered closing the blinds. There was no point. My room could've been as dark as Gran's grave, and sleep still would've avoided me.

Outside, a car drove past, its headlights forcing the shadows that had been cast on the walls to rise and then drop back into place as the car turned away.

Daddy's funeral. That's what the rapid rise and fall of the shadows reminded me of. The honor guard, pointing their rifles in the air, firing a volley, and lowering them again with precision.

Daddy had been strong. He could do anything he set his

mind to. When I was a little kid, I always imagined him in a super-hero outfit, even though most of the time he wore camouflage. But on special occasions, he'd wear his dress blues.

Up to the day of the funeral, part of me clung to the hope Daddy would appear and make our world right again—just like Superman always did. But he didn't, and Daddy was buried in his blue suit. He looked exactly like a superhero to me.

Only I didn't think superheroes could die.

Gramps stepped into Daddy's place. He'd never replace Daddy, but he was darn close. And Tick... He had helped to dislodge the sadness. But now he helped take Gramps away. He could blame it on the district attorney if he wanted, but it wasn't the lawyer who put my gramps in the back seat of a squad car. I'd already lost Dad. Was I going to lose Gramps too?

I flopped onto my pillow. The conversation in the kitchen with Gramps played over and over in my head. I wanted to turn it off and fall asleep, but I could no more do that than fold a butter-fly back into its cocoon. What did he mean by "settling things quiet-like"? And that weird comment about taking whatever steps necessary to make sure that he'd "never again have the same problem with that person"? And the unfamiliar look in his eyes. Cold and faraway.

Something about that chewed at my brain, but I couldn't...

Never again.

I sat up in bed.

Tick had asked if Gramps and Tabby were having problems...
I shuddered.

You didn't get much more "quiet-like" than poison. And you sure wouldn't have the same problem again. Not if you poisoned someone.

Surely that's not what he meant, though. Was it? I bit the inside of my lip. Then again, what did I know for sure about Gramps?

He'd been acting like a horse with a burr under its saddle ever since the discovery of Tabby's ring. I could understand being shocked by the news, but edgy and gruff?

Mama and I had lived with him for the past five years, but he *never* talked about his past. Even Mama said she didn't know a whole lot. Who was he *really*?

A tornado of doubts and questions whirled through my head, but I couldn't quiet them.

Tabby...no, my *gran* had been so young when she died. Younger even than Daddy. At least he knew the risks of fighting for his country. *She* was just living her life. If Daddy were still alive, I had no doubt he'd consider it his duty to find his mother's killer.

Gran needed justice.

And, as much as I wanted to believe Gramps was innocent,

I needed truth. Daddy wasn't here. That meant it was my duty to find her killer.

No matter what road the truth may lead me down.

I grabbed my pillow from behind my back and punched some air into it before flopping down to face the ceiling. Maybe things would look better tomorrow if tomorrow would just get here. I closed my eyes and attempted to convince myself to sleep. What was it adults always said? *The sooner you go to sleep, the sooner tomorrow will come…*or something like that.

Only, what if tomorrow brought something worse?

I might as well have tried getting warm using a wet blanket. Sleep wasn't going to come anytime soon. I crept downstairs to the kitchen for a glass of warm milk.

After getting my drink I carried it to the living room and twisted the tiny knob on the lamp that stood on the side table, bathing the room with soft light. I pulled Tabby's journal from my backpack and read.

I don't know what time I fell asleep. But when I woke, the journal was still on my lap, and my whole body ached with cramped muscles I'd earned from a restless night on the sofa.

CHAPTER 18

I WAS NEVER HAPPIER TO have been suspended from school than I was that Wednesday. The last thing I wanted was to face anyone, especially Beau. I had no doubt the gossip grapevine of Windy Bottom had already taken root, sprouted its thick limbs, and branched out with the news the police had searched our house and hauled Gramps in for questioning.

I was sitting on the front porch drawing in the dirt with a broken stick when Tick's police cruiser pulled into the driveway early the next morning. Gramps slammed both the car door and house door before Tick had even climbed fully out of his seat. Tick held his hat in one hand and ran his other hand over his face.

With a groan he sank and joined me on the porch. "I think it's safe to say your gramps is mad at me."

I stared straight ahead. "He's not the only one."

"I'm sorry, Coop, but Gomez had to do his job." He spoke quietly, as if he was afraid his words would send me into a door-slamming frenzy like Gramps. "I want to believe Doc's innocent, I really do." He ran his hand over his brow. "But the evidence—it's leading in a different direction. And oftentimes *it is* the spouse that…" He didn't finish his sentence.

I refused to look at him.

"Just 'cause Gramps was married to Tabby and owned a typewriter doesn't mean he's the murderer. Plus, what about Earl's blood on her ring? Or the fact her emerald necklace went missing? Huh?" I said.

Tick shoulders dropped. His forehead creased in worry lines. "We're trying to track down Earl." He sighed. "Your gramps had means, motive, and opportunity, and, between you and me, that's all the DA is focused on. I'm afraid it's only a matter of time…" He didn't finish his sentence.

"You're wrong." I stood and looked down at him. "I'm going to prove it."

~~~~

I spent the rest of the morning blasting Beethoven's Fifth and putting together a case board—one of those things detectives on TV use to display photos of the victim, crime scene, and suspects.

Technically, mine wasn't exactly a case *board*. More of a case closet. I'd shoved all my clothes to one side and taped what little information I had to the wall:

- Both pictures of Gran from the attic—the one on the tarmac with Gramps, and the one I'd taken on my phone where she's wearing the emerald necklace
- My copy of the fake (?) goodbye letter
- Gramps's torn-up photo with the *I'm sorry, Never Again* message on the back
- My list of questions I'd written earlier.

Then I made a suspect list.

Earl. Where was he? His blood was on her ring. He had a criminal record and a love of jewelry. To top it off, a quick Google search showed undertakers used arsenic to embalm bodies...or at least used to. Comforted Souls Funeral parlor had been around forever. Couldn't there have been arsenic hanging around?

I wanted a photo to hang next to his name—that's how the police did it. I found two. One was his old mug shot found online, and the other a half-page advertisement for Comforted Souls Funeral Parlor from the phone book. I opted for the mug shot and taped it to the closet wall.

I'd been reading up on arsenic. Being both tasteless and

odorless, it could've been slipped into anything Gran ate or drank the day she died. That meant Earl had motive, means, *and* opportunity. But one suspect wasn't much. I needed more, because I wasn't about to write: *Gramps*.

Next, I came up with a plan. The first part was to talk to people who were close to Gran when she was alive. Maybe one of them had a reason to want her dead or knew someone who did.

- *Burma*. He and Gramps had been friends since they were kids. Plus, he was right about news just walking into his shop and making itself comfortable in the chairs. If there was something going on forty years ago worth killing for, I had no doubt I'd hear about it at Burma's Cut 'N' Curl.
- *The Feather sisters.* Nothing happened in Windy Bottom without them being aware of it.

Sadly, hope of finding *something* incriminating in Gran's journal was disappearing faster than fried chicken at a church picnic. I was nearly halfway through reading it, but wasn't holding my breath.

Part two of my plan was trickier. As far as I could tell, the police weren't even looking for any other typewriters. They'd only taken Gramps's. If I could find the typewriter the letter was written on, it might lead me to the real murderer. I just wasn't sure how to put that one into action. I knew it was a long shot, but long shots were all I had.

Help from Liberty and Justice would've been perfect. While I was relieved I didn't have to be around Beau, it was a lousy time to be grounded. Then again, is there ever a good time?

CHAPTER 19

A COUPLE YEARS AGO WHEN our next-door neighbor, Mr. Wallace, went on to receive his heavenly reward, Mama remarked that deaths in Windy Bottom were treated just like births. People brought over food, then stuck around asking questions like *how's the family adjusting* and *is everyone sleeping all right?*

So it came as no surprise, once word got out that Tabby's funeral was in the making, that I spent my first full day of suspension watching people trail in and out of our house like ants at a picnic, their arms loaded with food, their mouths jam-packed with advice, and their minds no doubt overflowing with questions and assumptions about Gramps.

And I could hardly blame them.

The Gordons were minding the bookstore so Mama and

Gramps could work on funeral arrangements. Though, most of the arranging had been left to Mama for the time being. After Tick had dropped him back home, Gramps had left for some "alone time." Mama told him a drive in the country was just what he needed and not to worry about us.

Around three o'clock in the afternoon, when Mama couldn't bring herself to answer one more doorbell or knock, it became my job.

Justice grinned when I opened the door. "Nice shiner."

I reached up and gingerly touched my eye. "Yeah—it's pretty sore."

"I'll bet," said Liberty, rubbing her baseball against her jeans.

I leaned against the doorframe. "Y'all know I'm grounded for the rest of my life, right? I can't hang out."

"We know," said Justice. "We're just here to drop off something for your mama." He waved a pastry box. "From our folks."

"Apple turnovers from the café?" I asked, crossing my fingers. They were Mama's favorite. Maybe they'd put her in a better mood.

"Does a horse spit?" said Justice.

"Uh…no." I looked at Liberty, who just shook her head. "But a llama does."

"Close enough." He stepped around me into the house, his

backpack brushing my shoulder. "You've should've heard Beau today." He walked toward the kitchen. "Crowing like a prize rooster about how he *knew* the police would figure things out about your grandpa." He paused. "On second thought, it's probably best you weren't there after all."

Liberty tailed him.

"You think?" I scoffed and followed. "Anyway, the police have hardly 'figured things out.' They're trying to nail Gramps for the murder, which is totally screwed up. Or at least the DA is…according to Tick."

They both stopped and stared wide-eyed in the kitchen doorway at the food that covered every available surface. Mama stood in the center of the room looking lost.

"Wow. That's quite the haul." Lib tossed her baseball in the air and caught it, then pointed to the kitchen table. "I see you scored another one of Mrs. Alcott's German chocolate cakes."

"Two in one week." Justice grinned. "Bravo, Mrs. Goodman."

Mama rolled her eyes.

I nudged Justice. "I'm thinking I'll have some for breakfast."

"Wrong, mister." Mama faced me. "You're still in trouble— there's no cake for you."

"Speaking of breakfast, Miss Delilah," Liberty grabbed the box from her brother and handed it to Mama. "These are from our folks."

Mama's eyes lit up as she took them. "Apple turnovers?"

Justice smiled. "Does a horse—"

Liberty kicked him. "Yes ma'am, your favorite. And Mama says she's sorry she can't be here for support. Aunt Leslie just went into labor with her first baby, and Mama's flying out tonight to help her." She elbowed me and grinned. "Which means I don't have to go to the Generational Tea. I dodged that bullet."

Mama's eyes teared up. "Please tell them thank you. They are a godsend." She waved toward the counter. "I'll take turnovers from a friend over a three-course meal from a gossipmonger any day of the week."

The turnovers seemed to have cheered her. Maybe she'd loosen up the restrictions.

I cleared my throat. "Mama? Can Lib and Jus stay for a couple minutes? Please? I need to talk—"

"Nope."

She didn't even let me finish.

"You have one more day of suspension." She poked me lightly in the chest. "And, unlike today, you'll be spending it at the bookstore washing dishes."

I hung my head. "Gramps already told me."

She tussled my hair, then scowled. "*After* you get a haircut. With everything that's happened, we never did get you a trim before school started."

A haircut? Perfect! I could start on my list and talk to Burma.

Mama puffed out her cheeks. "And speaking of hair, the three of you need to get out of mine. Lib, Jus, please tell your folks thank you. These turnovers mean the world. Coop, back upstairs and do your schoolwork. And, Lord help me, if *one more* person walks through that front door, I'm going to—"

"Yoo-hoo! Delilah, dear," Miss Ruth's voice called out from the hall. "I brought you a batch of my fried chicken and some banana pudding. Plus, a jar of my best homemade mustard!"

Justice made a face. Miss Ruth's love for spicy mustards was as powerful as a Baptist preacher's love for revival. And the heat in some of them could make you think you hadn't quite made it through the pearly gates.

Mama ran her hand over her face and muttered. The food on the counter was already threatening to slide in an avalanche of fresh green beans, jars of sweet tea, and six different casseroles—not to mention Mrs. Alcott's German chocolate cake. She looked heavenward. "Lord, give me strength."

Justice leaned toward her. "Might be a good idea to ask for more counter space while you're at it."

Mama pointed a finger toward the door. "Out! Now!"

We passed Miss Ruth on her way to the kitchen. When we reached the front door, Justice spun around and glanced over my shoulder. "I got something for you." He swung his backpack off and dropped to his knees. Unzipping it, he reached in and handed me a folder. "The photographs from your gran's camera. I made them nice and big."

Yes! Finally!

"Dude. You're the best," I whispered excitedly. Gramps would be so happy, and if there were some of Dad, so would Mama.

Justice stood and jammed his hands in his pockets. "Wait till you see 'em."

I fumbled for the folder and flipped through picture after picture. My hopes disintegrated. "Stained glass windows? Flowers?" I looked at Liberty and Justice. "That's it?" I quickly thumbed through the rest. "What the heck am I supposed to do with these?"

"I'm pretty sure those windows are the ones up at Windy Bottom Baptist," said Justice. "Maybe she thought they were pretty or something?"

Liberty shrugged. "I'm sorry, Coop. I know you were hoping for…well, really *anything* other than stained glass windows, floral arrangements, and books."

I scowled. "Books?"

She nodded toward the stack in my hand. "Yeah. The last two were of a couple books next to each other."

I pulled them out. One showed the cover of two notebooks. No words, just *1977* stamped on front. The books were open in the other picture. The pages filled with columns and rows. Dates, numbers, and weird things like *memorial fund*, *expenses*, *deposits*, were written in different columns. I closed my eyes and sighed. "What a waste."

Miss Ruth's voice floated from the kitchen.

Justice looked past my shoulder and down the hall. "We better go. If your mama catches us still here, you won't be the only one grounded."

I dragged myself upstairs, tossed the folder on my desk, then flopped onto my bed and stared at the ceiling. I pounded my bed with my fists. Stained glass window and flowers? Seriously? Sure, the stained glass windows were pretty. And I *guess* women liked to take pictures of flowers. But books? Why those? I pushed myself up and sloughed through the pictures on my desk until I found them.

I had no idea what the numbers all meant. The only one that made sense was the date, Wednesday, March 23. That was the day before she died. Muttering, I added the photos to the case closet. Maybe they'd make sense later.

That night, after dinner and after Gramps had gone to his room, I got on my laptop and typed in words from the book photographs. *Expenses* and *deposits*. My screen filled with articles on accounting, balance sheets, and ledgers. I scanned them and clicked on the article that had a photo of a book kinda like the one from the camera.

A ledger. So that's what the books filled with columns and numbers were. Interesting. I read on but the article didn't mention why someone would keep two different ledgers for the same year. I typed my question into the search bar.

A half-hour later I flopped back against my chair and let out a huge breath, then grabbed my phone and called Justice.

"Put me on speaker so Liberty can hear," I said. "But keep the volume low. I want to keep it secret."

"Shut my door, Lib," Justice said.

"We're good," Liberty called. "What's up?"

"I researched those weird photos with the columns and numbers—ledgers, actually." I said. "You won't believe this, but I think someone was doctoring the books."

"What's that mean?" asked Justice.

"It means someone was embezzling. Stealing money from the"—I ran my finger ran up the description column of the ledger photo—"Memorial Fund."

"Stealing? From the church?" Liberty swore under her breath. "Who'd do that? How can you tell?"

"Remember how there were two ledgers for the same year?"

"Yeah."

"I compared them. There are different amounts in the same

account. One of the ledgers is the real one. It shows how much money the church *actually* received—that's the one the crook usually keeps. The other one is fake—that's the one everyone else sees."

One of them whistled. Probably Justice, which was what he did whenever math confused him.

"What are you going to do now?" asked Liberty.

"If we can find out who the bookkeeper for the church was all those years ago, maybe we'll discover the thief. I'll email Pastor Joel and see what he knows. I'll let you know what he says."

I said goodbye and wrote a short email to Pastor Joel at Windy Bottom Baptist. I didn't want to wait until Sunday.

Hi Pastor Joel,

Random question: Who was the bookkeeper at church 40 years ago?

Thanks—Coop Goodman

Then I grabbed my list of questions and a pen. Now I had *three* mysteries to solve.

7. Who was stealing from the church's memorial fund?

8. Who was the bookkeeper at Windy Bottom Baptist forty years ago?

9. Did Gran's death have anything to do with the stolen money?

CHAPTER 20

THURSDAY'S SUNRISE PIERCED THROUGH THE kitchen curtains as Mama stood by the sink in her pajamas and washed out her coffee mug. "The dishwasher hose at the bookstore needs replacing, Harley. Mr. Gordon said the dang thing leaked all day yesterday."

Gramps nodded. "I'll handle it. I want that contraption in working order, since Coop will be all but married to it today."

"After my haircut," I reminded him, dropping ice cubes into my own steaming cup of coffee. "And who knows, Burma may be real busy. Might take him a while to get to me."

"Don't you wish." Gramps grunted and hurried off to his room.

"Oh, Burma's will be busy," said Mama, handing me an apple turnover.

Cake for breakfast still wasn't an option, but apparently the fire in her anger had been doused enough to share a pastry.

"I've no doubt every chair will be filled with people sharing what they know, what they've heard, or what they've invented. Sending you into his shop is like sending Daniel into the lion's den," continued Mama. "But there's no hope for it. You look absolutely ragged, and you don't want *me* cutting your hair. 'Sides, at least it will show everyone that life goes on and we're doing all right."

The late morning air was warm and the sun perched above the newly painted Dollar Daze sign as I walked down Willow Avenue toward Burma's Cut 'N' Curl. I rounded the corner of the bank and almost ran into a line of customers that stretched out the door of A Latté Books—something that hadn't happened since its grand opening a few years back. Mama hadn't been kidding when she'd said people would be coming out of the woodwork. Especially now that Gramps was the prime suspect.

On the other side of the long line, the door to Burma's shop stood open, letting the morning air in and the gossip out. I didn't want anyone stopping me, so I tugged my baseball cap farther down and I hurried on.

I peered through the front window of the Cut 'N' Curl. Mama

was right—every seat was full. Not that Burma had a lot of seats, but still. Willy the postman stood in the waiting area jabbering with Old Elmer, who sat with his cane in the swivel chair closest to the counter. Burma stood behind the other swivel chair and snipped at the few pieces of hair Gunner Creedy still had left.

Miss Velma and Mrs. Alcott, their hair wound into pink rollers, rested under hair dryers, shouting at each other to be heard over the hum of the machines. A stranger might mistakenly think Burma had opened his doors an hour ago in order to have two ladies already under dryers plus a man in the chair, but us town folk knew different. Miss Velma and Mrs. Alcott were known to roll their hair at home and then spend the morning under Burma's dryers shooting the breeze. And as long as a paying customer didn't need to dry their hair, Burma was happy to oblige.

Snippets of conversations rode the shampoo-and-perm-scented air onto the sidewalk to where I stood.

"…heard poison was what done her in. And the police…"

"…never did think she ran off…leave a baby?"

"—that's a load of hogwash. Millie said…"

"…anyone seen Earl lately? Rumor has it…"

"Yes, but Wendell mentioned… And 'sides…"

"—think about it. Tabby, Steven, now Doc…bad things… family's cursed."

I'd been counting on the fact gossip would flow at Burma's Cut 'N' Curl. Hopefully, I'd learn something. But now, hearing it made the excitement that had been burning in my stomach turn to ash. I didn't know if I was embarrassed or angry they were talking about Gramps and Gran. Probably a bit of both.

But I had to go in—not only for my haircut, but to try to clear Gramps's name.

I stepped through the doorway and the talking continued. As soon as I took off my cap though, the conversations fell to the floor with a thud.

Only the hair dryers continued to drone on. The ladies' faces matched their pink rollers. I wasn't sure who was more red, them or me. But the heat I felt in my cheeks could've dried everyone's hair.

"Morning, Coop." Burma looked up from Gunner's head. "Come on in." He paused. "How's Harley holding up?"

"Fine." I forced myself to smile.

Old Elmer swiveled his chair to face me and jabbed his cane toward my feet. "The police any closer to finding out who done it yet? Do they have any other suspects besides Doc?"

"When's the funeral?" Miss Velma bellowed over the dryer's whir.

"Mama and Gramps are still working on it," I hollered back.

Gunner stretched out of the chair. "Nice shiner, Coop." He

pointed to my eye. "I heard of all the people to wallop, you chose Beauregard Knapp." He examined his wisps of hair in the mirror. "Go big or go home, right? Or in your case you went big *and* you went home." He laughed at his joke and wandered out the door after leaving money on the counter.

I turned to Burma. "I need a haircut. Mama's orders."

He gave me the once-over and nodded. "Well, there's Willy and then Elmer—"

"No, no—let Coop go first." Willy pushed me into the empty chair. "We can wait, can't we, Elmer?"

"I've nowhere to go but here. Now"—Old Elmer repositioned himself to face me and spoke to my reflection in the mirror—"how are you doing?"

"Yeah." Willy sidled up next to him. "Anything…uh…new?"

Miss Velma reached up, turned off her dryer, and lifted the top.

Mrs. Alcott did the same and shook her finger at Willy and Elmer. "A gossip's mouth is the devil's postbag."

Willy spun around. "There's no need for you to act high and mighty. We all heard you gabbing on just now. Devil's postbag." He scoffed. "Devil's handbag more like."

"*Harrumph.*" She wrenched open a magazine but didn't turn her dryer back on.

Miss Velma popped herself out of her chair and joined

Elmer, Willy, and Burma. The four of them stared expectantly at me in the mirror.

I gulped.

Burma *tsk-tsked* as he wrapped a strip of tissue paper around my neck, which was almost as scratchy as any loose hair would've been.

"At least let me ask him about his hair before y'all start pummeling him with questions." Picking up his scissors, he chuckled. "Mind you, I'm a mite curious myself. Same cut as last time, Coop?"

I nodded. "Burma, can I ask you something?"

"Sure." He grinned and leaned over. "You got girl troubles?" He winked at me in the mirror.

I snorted. "No. It's about Gramps."

He looked at my reflection. "I hope you're not worried, son. Your gramps is a good man."

Suds nodded. "He don't drink, don't smoke. Don't cuss, either. Not unless you count that time the leaf blower caught fire." He patted my shoulder. "Based on the slew of swear words that flew from his mouth I wasn't sure if he was even allowed to be a deacon at church anymore."

Mrs. Alcott lowered her magazine. "That doesn't mean he's perfect."

Miss Velma shushed her.

I focused my attention on Burma. "It's just that for someone who's practically like my dad, I don't know much about him from before we came. He's not one for talking about the past. Y'all have known each other for years, right?"

"Best friends growing up." *Snip, Snip, Snip.*

I knew that. "Yeah. I just meant…"

"We were downright inseparable until he left for college."

"And after college?"

"Well… Things got mighty tense for a bit when he came home."

"Really? What happened? Y'all had a fight?" I blurted. At least it was a better blurt than *did you kill his wife?*

Willy nudged Old Elmer and grinned. "Did they fight?"

Burma chuckled. "It was the *only* fight Harley and I had, but it was a doozy. Almost destroyed our friendship."

Willy leaned in. "They both loved the same girl."

Wait. What?

I gawked at Burma in the mirror. "Nah-uh."

Miss Velma's rollers jiggled as she nodded. "Yes—it's true."

"Wait—you loved Tabby too?"

Burma ran the comb through my hair and trimmed the ends.

Willy grinned. "Oh, son, I don't mean your grandma. She came on the scene later."

Elmer shifted in the chair and poked my arm. "Ruth Feather."

My jaw dropped. "Shut the front door!"

Elmer eyed the door, puzzled. "It *is* shut."

Burma placed both hands on my shoulders and looked at me in the mirror. "My sweet Ruth was in love with your gramps, much to my dismay. Nearly ruined our friendship."

"That woman's one rocking chair short of a front porch," muttered Old Elmer.

Burma shook his scissors to him. "You're just jealous she bakes lemon pound cake for me and not you."

Old Elmer grunted.

"So," I cleared my throat. "What happened?"

He smiled. "I first laid eyes on Ruth Feather when I was fourteen years old. Her family had just moved to Windy Bottom."

"Poorer than church mice too," piped Mrs. Alcott from behind her magazine.

Willy thumbed toward Mrs. Alcott. "*Devil's handbag,*" he mouthed.

"I didn't care about that." Burma scowled. "The three of us became good friends, but I could tell she had a thing for your gramps. Harley was a looker, smart, and destined for big things. She was smitten with him." He poked me in the shoulder. "Pay attention to that. You can tell a lot by the way a girl looks at you."

"Yes sir." No girls were looking at me so I didn't need to know. I wished he'd hurry up and get to the important stuff.

"Harley gave her his word they'd marry when he got back from medical school. He—"

Miss Velma nudged Burma aside. "He even got on his knee and gave her a promise ring."

"What's a promise ring?" I asked.

Her brows pinched together. "Well, dear, it's like an engagement ring, sort of."

Gramps had *promised* to marry Miss Ruth? Whoa. I'd always kind of viewed her as a grandma of sorts. But if she had married Gramps, she really would've *been* my grandma.

"Anyway," Burma moved to my other side and continued snipping, "she got her teaching degree and returned to Windy Bottom and waited for Harley. Then one day, he returns with a doctor's degree in his hand and a wedding ring on his finger."

"And a city girl on his arm," added Mrs. Alcott. She dropped the magazine into her chair and marched over to us. "The news was enough to make people forget to sweeten their tea."

Burma nodded.

Gramps had jilted Miss Ruth?!

Miss Velma sighed. "Poor girl was inconsolable. And Meriwether." She shook her head. "Well, she was fit to be tied, wasn't she? You know how protective she can be."

Willy chuckled. "A mama bear with a hunted cub looked tame next to Meriwether."

Old Elmer grunted. "If you ask me, Ruth's bolts got turned that day and she hasn't been right since."

Could sweet old Miss Ruth have been capable of murder all those years ago? Sure, I could see Miss Meriwether having murderous tendencies...but Miss Ruth?

Burma ignored him and continued. "Vowed she'd never love another. I was furious with Harley for treatin' her that way." I could see his lips pinched together in the mirror as he leaned over to trim my neckline.

Okay, wait. Maybe Burma was the murderer! "What did you do?" I croaked.

"You wanted to knock him clear 'cross Tipton County." Willy slapped his arm across Burma's back and wheezed out a laugh.

Burma straightened up. "I'm trying to cut his hair, not his neck!"

"Sorry." He stepped back.

Burma grinned. "Love can make you do some wild things."

"Like what?" I breathed.

"Nuthin! Whaddya think, I punched him? I realized your gramps had done me a favor, and maybe now I had a chance with Ruth."

"Not likely," muttered Mrs. Alcott.

"Crazy bat," said Old Elmer.

I stared at him for a second, trying to figure out if he meant Burma or Mrs. Alcott.

Miss Velma nudged Burma away again. "But Ruth took the high road. She made it a point to befriend your grandma, even though it must've been difficult for her to see Doc each day, knowing what could've been."

"You mean what *should've* been." Mrs. Alcott huffed. "He broke his promise to her." She turned *broke* into a two-syllable word.

Burma placed both hands on Miss Velma and scooted her off to the side.

"What about you and Gramps? Did y'all ever set things right?"

He nodded. "Yuppers." *Snip. Snip. Snip.* He stood back and admired his handiwork. "It's hard to be mad at someone just because they fell in love." He unfastened the cape and whipped it off me. "Done! 'Sides, I've had years to woo Ruth, and I think she's finally beginning to see what a fine catch I am."

Old Elmer shook his head. "You're as loony as she is."

I stretched out of the chair. "Thanks, Burma—for everything."

I'd walked in wanting to find out what was going on back then, and, boy, did I ever.

CHAPTER 21

GRAMPS CLOSED HIS TOOLBOX AS I came through the back kitchen door of A Latté Books.

"Perfect timing." His arm swept to the counter behind him. Racks filled with dirty plates and mugs were stacked like the Leaning Tower of Pisa. "We're almost out of clean dishes, and there've been so many people, we're on our last gallon of milk. Mr. Gordon had to run to Piggly Wiggly to get more. He just got back."

"I saw the line on my way to Burma's." I pointed behind him. "You forgot your screwdriver."

He grabbed it and tossed it into the box. "Your mama and Mr. Gordon haven't had two minutes to catch their breath." He snapped the latch shut. "This cursed dishwasher's taken up my whole morning. I replaced the hose and just ran a test rack through. Let's see how she fared."

He slid the dishwasher door open and a thunderhead of steam billowed toward us. Vapory fingers clung to the hot mugs in the rack as he pulled it across the stainless steel counter.

Gramps squeezed my shoulder. "Looks like she'll live to work another day—just like you." He tossed me an apron.

"Should I take this clean rack out to Mama?"

He shook his head. "I'm headed to the front lines. I'll take it with me. Your hair looks nice, by the way."

"Thanks."

Gramps hoisted the rack and carried it toward the front. He whistled a tune as he disappeared through the swinging door. I hadn't heard Gramps whistle in a while. He was probably doing it more for my sake than his. I knew he was worried about how I was dealing with everything, and my fight with Beau hadn't exactly eased his mind.

I tugged the apron over my head. For the next two hours, I pushed and pulled racks loaded with dirty plates and mugs in and out of the steamy box. No sooner would I set a stack of clean dishes on the counter, than Mama, or Gramps, or Mr. Gordon would swap it out for a tub of dirty ones. The kitchen turned into a steam bath, and as much as I hated to wear the heavy rubber dishwashing gloves, I finally pulled them on to protect what was left of my fingerprints.

Each time the swinging door swung open and shut with a

thwop, voices from the front whooshed into the kitchen. But only bits and pieces reached my ears.

"...I'm holding up just fine, thanks..."

"...Yes...a homicide. No, we don't know anything new. I'm sure..."

"Thank you...we're still working on funeral arrangements..."

"No, I *did not* spend the night locked in the pokey...Honestly, what—"

"Anyone laid eyes on Earl yet?"

And on it continued.

Mama pushed through the door just after the clock flipped to 2:30 and sighed. Wisps of hair had fallen from her ponytail, and her apron had at least seven fresh coffee stains. Usually Thursdays were a two-stain kind of day.

"Thank goodness it's slowed to a trickle," she said. "I like the business, but if I hear from one more 'concerned citizen,' I'll scream."

My stomach rumbled. I pulled the rubber gloves off and draped them over the sink faucet.

"Can I grab a sandwich and a cookie? I'm starving."

"Sure." Mama sank into the chair in the office. "Grab one for me too. But I want a brownie, not a cookie. I deserve it after this morning."

I pushed through the door into the bookstore. Gramps disappeared down the hall to the storeroom. Mr. Gordon rested on a stool behind the counter, fanning himself with a takeout menu. He gave me a weak wave and smile.

"I'm grabbing lunch for Mama." I walked to the refrigerated case that held pastries and sandwiches for sale and slid it open. "Do you want anything?"

He puffed out his cheeks and thought. "I'll take a cookie—but don't tell Mrs. Gordon when she gets back from her sister's—she's trying to put me on a diet."

"Your secret's safe with me."

I handed him his cookie and then delivered Mama her food. I came back out front to eat with Mr. Gordon. A sense of peace settled across the room. The chaos of earlier was gone.

Only Mrs. Sumner, Windy Bottom's oldest citizen, and her daughter, Andrea Grace, remained. They sat in their chairs near the front bay window.

Moments later, the bell rang as the door was pushed open. Angus Knapp, Beau's daddy, staggered drunkenly through the doorway and stumbled into the coffee table in front of the sofa.

"Goodman!" Angus shouted. "Where are you? Wanna talk to you!"

"You've got to be kidding me," Mr. Gordon muttered. "Stay here, Coop." He rounded the counter. "We're about to close, Angus." He braced Mr. Knapp under his elbow and turned him around toward the door.

Mrs. Sumner and Andrea Grace gawked at Angus, mouths open.

Mr. Gordon, being taller and heavier than Angus, wasn't someone to be trifled with, but Angus had just enough liquor in him to be dangerous.

"Get your hands off me." He wrestled his arm away from Mr. Gordon and poked him in the chest. "I'm not going anywhere."

Andrea Grace set her coffee down, stood, and shifted her mother's chair and then her own, to better watch the scene unfolding before them.

Gramps walked in from the storeroom. "What's going on?"

"I got every right to be here." Angus's words slurred together. He smoothed down his shirt.

Mr. Gordon made eye contact with me. "Call Vidler."

Angus's legs wobbled as he teetered toward the counter. How he was able to make it through the maze of chairs and side tables without falling over anything else—or himself—was astonishing.

Angus glared at me through bloodshot eyes.

Gramps moved between us. "Leave him alone, Angus."

My fingers fumbled to punch the numbers on the phone.

Tick's voice sounded at the other end of the phone. "This is Vidler."

I placed my hand near the mouthpiece. "Tick—Angus is really drunk. Angry. He's here. I mean, at the bookstore. Hurry."

"I'm on my way." He hung up.

Gramps took a deep breath. "Why are you here, Angus?"

"Should've known my Cordelia wasn't the first." He leaned into Gramps's face.

Gramps waved away his breath and stepped back. "Okay, Angus, sit down."

Mr. Gordon shook his head. "I'll get him a black coffee." He walked behind Gramps and joined me.

Angus pushed off the counter. "My wife. *Your* wife. Suppose that makes you a serial killer, don't it?" He waved his arm around. "Got any more bodies out there, Goodman?"

The vein in Gramps's neck twitched.

Mama pushed through the kitchen door.

Concern pressed into her brow. "What's going on out here?"

"Ain't been the same since my Cordelia... Gonna get you for that..." Angus fell against the counter and broke into ugly sobs.

Mama's eyes darted from Gramps to Angus, then back to Gramps.

"Come on, Angus. I'll drive you home." Gramps pulled Angus off the counter.

"No!" Angus's face, already the shade of plums, deepened further in color. "You're a wife killer!" Spittle flew from his mouth.

Gramps's jaw tightened. "You're desperate, Angus. I didn't kill anybody." His voice was low and tight.

"Liar!"

His hand curled into a fist as he drew his arm back.

Mama yelled.

Mr. Gordon ran around the counter.

Angus swung.

Gramps ducked.

Angus tripped on the edge of the rug and collided with a floor lamp. He fell, striking his head on the solid wood table on his way down. He twitched a couple times on the floor, then… nothing. A pool of red crept across the carpet.

"Angus!" Mama gripped the counter's edge and looked over.

Gramps rushed to where Angus lay. "Call 911!" He put his fingers on Angus's neck, feeling for a pulse. "He's not breathing. Coop, get me something to stop the bleeding."

Gramps tilted Angus's head back and started CPR.

The sight of the blood made the food in my stomach turn sour.

"Cooper! Now!" barked Gramps over his shoulder.

I grabbed the dish towel off the top of the counter and ran to Gramps, who was pushing down on Angus's chest.

"Hold it against his head, Coop."

Tick ran through the front door. "What's happened?"

"He fell and he's not breathing." Gramps blew into his mouth again. Angus's chest rose and fell with each of Gramps's breaths.

Gramps interlocked his fingers a third time and pressed down, counting quietly.

Tick thumbed toward his car. "Do you need a defibrillator?"

Angus groaned but didn't open his eyes.

"No." Gramps felt Angus's wrist and looked up at Tick. "He has a pulse. But it's weak."

Mrs. Sumner and Andrea Grace clung to each other's arms and watched from a distance.

Mama knelt next to me. She put her hands over the towel I pressed on Angus's head. "I've got this. Go wash your hands."

Blood had seeped through the towel. My red-stained hands shook.

Tick stepped back from where Angus lay and spoke into the walkie-talkie attached to his shoulder straps. He listened to the reply and gave some code. "The ambulance is close."

Angus's face was a pale gray color, a huge contrast from the angry purple-red it had been. A moan escaped from his lips and his eyes fluttered open. "Beau," he rasped.

"Lay still," Gramps said, taking over for Mama. "Coop—get me another towel."

"It's okay, Angus." Mama held his hand and stroked it.

Gramps kept his fingers on Angus's other wrist and his eyes on his watch. His lips moved, counting the heartbeats.

"Take care of Beau…" Angus closed his eyes again.

"Oh, sweet Jesus." Mama put her hand on her heart. "Is he...?"

"No," Gramps said. "Just unconscious."

I handed him a new towel. Everything inside me screamed *turn away*, but I couldn't.

The whine of the ambulance's sirens drew closer. Mr. Gordon dashed outside. Through the window I saw him wave them down.

Then I ran to the bathroom and threw up.

CHAPTER 22

"WHAT ABOUT BEAU?" I ASKED as the ambulance, lights and sirens on, disappeared around the corner.

Tick sighed. "There's no family in the area. I'll call Department of Children and Families."

"No." Mama said. "Don't send him to stay with total strangers. Not now." She shook her head. "Beau can stay with us."

The blood drained from my entire body. "Mama—"

"Hush." She narrowed her eyes at me. "It is the right thing to do."

No way. No way. No possible way.

Tick sighed. "Staying in town would be ideal, but I have to follow protocol..."

I closed my eyes. *Please Lord, yes, I promise to be good forever and ever.*

"Let me notify DCFS of the situation. I witnessed Angus asking you to look after Beau, and with the overload of cases DCFS has, that might be all we need…temporarily at least. But I have to call it in."

Mama nodded. "I understand."

I didn't. It took everything I had not to punch my fist through a wall. Beau, my enemy, my nemesis whose happiness depended on my misery, could become a houseguest?

Tick tugged on his hat and opened his car door. "Right now, I need to get Beau from school and take him to the hospital. I'll let you know about DCFS as soon as I can." He started to shut his door but stopped. "I'll need to get statements about what happened. Do you think we can all meet at your house this evening?"

"Of course," said Mama.

Gramps nodded, though the last thing he probably wanted was to give *another* statement to the police.

~~~~

Twilight hid its tail between its legs and skedaddled as dark clouds bullied their way across the sky. There was a promise of a gully washer within the hour as Mama, Gramps and I cleaned up after dinner.

Mama shut the refrigerator door with a sigh. "I never thought I'd say this, but thank you, Lord, for Mrs. Alcott and her infernal

Compassion League. Having all those leftovers from yesterday was a blessing after *today's* crisis." She checked her watch. "I'd better make up Beau's bed. Keith will be here with him soon."

She squeezed my shoulder as she passed by me. "Remember what we discussed."

It hadn't been much of a discussion.

When I had asked Mama where Beau would be sleeping, it was like she'd decided to punish me for all my screwups—past, present, and future.

"Your room."

My jaw dropped. "My room?"

"I don't expect you to like it, but I do expect you to Make. It. Work. This feud stops here and now." She'd punctuated the statement with her "I dare you to fight me on this" stare, complete with one arched eyebrow and a hand on her hip.

"I won't forget," I mumbled, carrying my spaghetti-smeared dinner plate to the sink. It wasn't like I could swallow anymore.

Lightning spider-webbed across the sky, and thunder grumbled in the distance. Usually I liked Thursday nights—on account of Friday being the next day. Fridays were the best. But I was *not* looking forward to tonight. Not with Beau being my roommate.

Gramps opened the dishwasher door and moved around to the other side. "How about you rinse and I'll load?"

I flipped the faucet on. Spaghetti sauce slid from the plates down the drain. The image reminded me of Angus's head, and I shuddered.

Gramps looked up from pouring himself a cup of coffee. "You all right?"

"Just keep seeing Mr. Knapp lying there…and the blood." I handed him the rinsed plates. "Will he be okay?"

"I hope so." Gramps set his coffee aside and stacked the plates in the dishwasher along with the silverware. "There're a lot of unknowns with head injuries. And now that he's slipped into a coma, it's even more up in the air."

A stubborn piece of lettuce had dried to the side of the salad bowl, refusing to be washed away. I picked at it. "Why was he so drunk?"

Gramps stepped on the trash can pedal and threw away two remaining pieces of garlic bread. We *never* had leftover garlic bread. Not before tonight anyway. But none of us seemed to have much of an appetite.

"Despair can lead us to do some desperate things. Angus has been self-medicating with alcohol for ages. But I've never seen him toasted by two o'clock in the afternoon. Stay away from the bottle, Coop. Nothing good ever comes from it."

"Yes, sir."

He ran his hands back and forth through his hair. It stuck

up in odd places. "I guess this mess with Tabby hit a nerve and brought back too many painful memories of *his* wife. It would be like throwing gasoline on a raging fire."

"Yeah, but when Gran ran away—or died—you didn't go ballistic like he did." Then again what did I really know? I looked at him. "Did you?"

"Tragedy affects different people in different ways." He picked up his coffee cup and gazed into it. "I was heartbroken, but I managed. However, I chalk that up more to the people around me. Our family's lived in Windy Bottom since it was established. I had friends that helped me cope."

I held up a clean salad bowl. "Yeah, but the Knapps have lived here a long time and knew people too, right?"

Gramps tossed me the towel from his shoulder. "Angus has always been bitter, and bitterness doesn't produce friends. Cordelia was beginning to pull him out of it, but when she died, Angus had no one. He was mad with grief and funneled all his anger toward me."

"Why you?"

Gramps shrugged. "Because I couldn't save her. I understood all too well what he was going through, so I didn't let it bother me, but," he sighed, "I see now how it's taken its toll on you...and Beau."

I nodded. "Beau's just as mean as his daddy."

Gramps looked up over the top of his mug before taking a sip. "Don't be quick to judge him. Beau's a victim twice over. Angus fell into a hole of anger when his wife passed, and he never climbed out. Maybe Beau figured the only way to be with his daddy was to join him down there."

"You can say that again," I muttered.

"Part of him died when Cordelia did." Gramps shut the dishwasher door. "And now with this injury, if Angus decides not to fight for his life, he just may lose it. He could wake tomorrow...or not at all."

"You mean he could die?" My stomach clenched.

"That's exactly what I mean."

I stared at Gramps. "What would happen to Beau?"

He shook his head. "I don't know." He stared back. "Just pray Angus recovers."

Beau never knew his mom. And if his daddy died... Well, that would be like what had happened to me, but double. As much as I disliked Beau, I wouldn't wish that on anybody. Not even him.

CHAPTER 23

THE ONLY GOOD THAT CAME from Angus's accident was Mama agreed Justice and Liberty could come over that night with Mr. Gordon. There was so much going on she seemed to have forgotten I was grounded.

Tick wanted anyone who saw what happened at the bookstore to meet at Gramps's house so he could take statements. Mrs. Sumner and Andrea Grace were already in the kitchen with Mama and Gramps. They'd arrived a few minutes ago holding a plate of rain-sprinkled chocolate chip cookies, missing the downpour by just a hair. Hopefully, the bad-tempered weather would make the others late and buy me more time.

At least now I could show Lib and Jus the case closet. Earlier

I had gone on the hunt for photos of my new suspects—Burma and both Feather sisters.

I sent up a quick thank-you to the good Lord that a couple years back the Windy Bottom Public Library had scanned all of the old issues of the *Windy Bottom Breeze* into a digital format. I'd found an article online of Burma standing with his arm draped across the shoulders of Miss Ruth at the opening of the library's new gazebo. After printing it, I took scissors and separated Burma from Miss Ruth. Sadly, his arm stayed with her.

But that's where my luck had run out. The only photo of Miss Meriwether was the size of a postage stamp from an old school yearbook.

I'd just finished adding the new photos alongside Earl's mug shot, when Justice's voice bellowed and footsteps thundered up the stairs. I yanked Gramps's torn-up wedding photo off the closet wall. I wasn't ready to show that to anyone. Not yet. I hid it in my desk drawer just as Justice walked in.

Liberty appeared behind him. "Hey, Coop."

Raindrops dripped from their hair.

Justice flopped down on my bed. "Dad told us Beau was gonna be staying at your house. Tough break!"

"Tell me about it," I grumped.

"Can't he stay with a relative or something?" asked Liberty.

I shrugged. "I guess there aren't any close by. Tick's bringing him over in a little bit. But I don't want to talk about him now. He'll ruin things soon enough when he actually shows up." I motioned them over and stepped aside, revealing the case closet. "Take a look."

"Whoa, cool." Justice stood riveted. "What is it?"

"My case notes on Gran's murder."

I'd written the suspect names above each picture. The names weren't needed, but they made it look official.

Liberty stepped closer to examine it. "This is awesome, Coop." She snorted. "Nice picture of Earl."

"The way I see it, we've got four suspects. Five, if you count Gramps—but I don't."

"Then why is his photo on the wall?" Justice asked.

"To prove he's innocent. Duh," said Liberty.

"These," I pointed to part of the wall, "are our suspects. Want to hear my theories?"

"Totally," said Liberty.

Justice nodded. "Shoot."

I pulled the cards I'd filled out earlier from my back pocket. "Suspect number one, Earl." I taped the notecard under his photo.

Suspect: Earl
Motive: Gran knew he was stealing?
Means: Embalming fluid (in muffins?)
Opportunity: ?

"When you told me earlier how Earl used to steal jewelry, it got me thinking. What if," I said, "he started stealing *more* than just jewelry, like money from the memorial fund, and Gran knew about it? He has to silence her or risk heading back to jail." I told them what I'd read about undertakers using arsenic a long time ago. "Working at the funeral parlor, he'd have tons of poisons to choose from. Then he stages it to look like a runaway, and steals her necklace—because old habits die hard."

"Makes sense," said Liberty. "Tabby had the proof on her camera, and based on the last entry in the ledgers, she died the next day. If that doesn't scream motive, I'll wear a dress."

I turned toward my desk and picked Gran's journal up. "I hadn't told y'all yet, but Gran's journal was mixed in with some of Dad's stuff."

"Her journal, huh?" Liberty took it from my hand and flipped through the pages. "That's cool! Does she mention Earl?"

I nodded. "Nothing incriminating yet, except he was always baking muffins even back then—which might be how he poisoned her. I'm not done reading, but if he *was* stealing, I'm hoping she wrote about it."

"She was a southpaw," said Liberty.

"A what?" I asked.

"She was left-handed." She pointed to the journal. "See how

the left side of each page always looks a little messy? That's from where her arm slid across the page as she was writing and the ink smeared. Happens to me all the time."

"Hey, back to Earl for a minute," said Justice. "How do you think his blood got on her ring?"

"I don't know."

I filled them in on everything I could remember from the Cut 'N' Curl that morning. Liberty pretended to gag when I got to the part about Gramps giving Miss Ruth a promise ring. But then again, her favorite part of *Romeo and Juliet* was when they both went belly-up.

"What if," I said, "Miss Ruth killed Gran hoping Gramps would eventually remarry her? In her mind then, everything goes back to how it should've been."

"But *you* said they were friends," Justice argued.

"So were Caesar and Brutus," Liberty said, "but Brutus still knifed him in the back. '*Et tu, Brute*' mean anything to you?"

"Not really," muttered Justice.

"Ruth is a suspect, but I sure hate thinking she's the murderer. She's practically my grandma, and I don't know how she would've gotten the arsenic." I added her card to the wall. "Plus, she's no bigger than a pickle, so I have a really hard time seeing her drag a body all the way to the playground and then burying it."

Suspect: Miss Ruth
Motive: Jealousy/Marriage
Means: ?—but no strength to drag a body
Opportunity: ?

"Agreed. We need someone with a car," said Liberty. "That's why Earl's the perfect suspect. He could've put the body in the back of his hearse, and no one would ever know. But as for arsenic, you know it's in rat poison, right?" said Liberty. "And back then you could buy it at the drugstore."

"What?" I stared at her.

"Yep." She walked over to my computer and typed something into the search bar.

"You sure 'bout that, Lib? How do you know?" asked Justice.

"Because I read. You should try it sometime," she said over her shoulder. "Pharmacists used to keep a list of everyone who bought the stuff. It was actually called a poison registry—kinda a cool name for it." Her fingers flew over the keys as she continued her search. "And if you know your way around the library, like yours truly, and you learn some awesome research skills, like yours truly, you can find that list. It's one of the many perks of helping out in the library." Moments later, Liberty leaned back in the chair, arms crossed and a smug smile plastered across her face. "Forget embalming fluid, Coop. According to this, the *whole* town owned arsenic."

"I'll be," I muttered, staring at the screen. Great. Yesterday I didn't have enough suspects, and today I had too many.

Justice leaned over Liberty's shoulder and then looked at me. "Kinda weird so many people in Windy Bottom bought rat poison around the same time, don't you think?"

I shrugged. "Maybe not. I remember an entry in Gran's journal about people seeing lots of rats once the Piggly Wiggly started to be built. The construction probably messed up their nesting grounds and stuff, and that's why the rats were out into the open."

Justice shuddered.

"Well," I said, "at least now I can fill in the *means* section on the rest of my suspect cards."

"Only if their names are on the poison registry, though. How far does that list go back?" Justice asked.

"A long time," said Liberty, turning back to the computer. "And I don't see Miss Ruth's name anywhere."

"But look." Justice jabbed a finger at the screen. "There's Miss Meriwether's name. And they live together, so Miss Ruth still could've used it."

"Good point," I said.

I grabbed a pencil and erased the question mark on Miss Ruth's card in the closet, then wrote *Rat Poison*. I did the same to the cards I held in my hand and glanced at the time. "I got to hurry before Beau gets here and ruins things." I taped Burma's card under his picture.

Suspect: Burma
Motive: Angry (for losing Miss Ruth)
Means: Rat Poison
Opportunity: ?

"Picture it," I continued. "Miss Ruth, the love of his life, vows to never love another. He's lost his chance. Burma blames Gramps. Maybe he decides that if he can't have *his* happily ever after, then Gramps shouldn't, either. He waits for Gramps to leave for the clinic, poisons Gran, fakes her disappearance, and types the letter."

Liberty tilted her head to the side, like she was weighing the validity of my theory. She shrugged. "I suppose it's possible."

"It's the weakest, but we can still check if he had an alibi." I held up a finger. "I have one more theory."

"Please tell me it's Miss Meriwether," said Justice. "To be as cranky as she is, she must've murdered *someone*."

Liberty flicked the back of his head with her finger. "Just because someone's grouchy, that doesn't make them a murder suspect."

"It does in my book," muttered Justice.

"Mine too." I taped up the last card.

Suspect: Meriwether Feather
Motive: Revenge

Means: Rat Poison

Opportunity: ?

"Revenge?" Liberty scrunched her nose.

"Think about it. Gramps totally jilted her little sister—the only person she actually *likes* in the whole town. Humiliated her. Left her at the altar, whatever you want to call it. And Miss Meriwether is overprotective *on steroids*. How many times have we overheard her at the bookstore telling Miss Ruth to put on a sweater, or take her vitamins, or not to eat a donut, or don't use artificial sweetener, or something else neurotic?"

They nodded.

"Miss Velma said Miss Meriwether was fit to be tied when Gramps stood her sister up," I said. "So maybe she kills Tabby, buries the body, and writes the note. Now Gramps has to live with the humiliation that *his wife* walked out on him—just like he walked out on Ruth."

Liberty blew her bangs from her face. "I can understand that as a motive for when Doc and Tabby first moved back to Windy Bottom. But after *two years?*" She shook her head. "Something must've happened for Meriwether to get a hankering for revenge if that's the case."

She made a little bit of sense, but I wasn't ready to let go of Miss Meriwether as a suspect. "People are like volcanoes.

Unpredictable. Who knows when they're going to explode? And, remember when the skeleton was first discovered, she tried to convince people it was from a family burial site," I said. "She *didn't want* people to know what she'd done."

"It's a stretch," said Justice. "But it *would* explain her cranky attitude and the fact she doesn't like you—since you're related to Doc."

"She doesn't like anybody," I said.

Liberty stood back and examined the case closet. "Well, my money's on dog-tag-stealing Earl. And if Earl *had* gone back to stealing jewelry—like Tabby's emerald necklace—maybe he still has it. If we found it, it'd be an open-and-shut case."

"Agreed," I said.

Liberty pointed to a different photo. "Is that your grandma?"

"No. *That's* Miss Ruth, only like, way younger."

Justice elbowed Lib aside and squinted at the picture. "She and your gran sure look a lot alike."

I leaned in. "I hadn't really noticed before but, yeah, you're right." I compared the photos of Miss Ruth and Gran. "Gran's taller, but they have the same hair color, and both could stand to eat a few cheeseburgers."

"Can't say that about Miss Meriwether, that's for sure," muttered Justice.

Miss Meriwether was built like a John Deere tractor.

"So what's the plan?" asked Liberty.

"We do what police do and question the suspects, only we don't want to spook the killer."

"I know!" Liberty said. "What if we say we're writing a tribute to Tabby for the school paper?"

Justice stared at her. "We have a school paper?"

"We do now." Liberty grinned.

"Lib, you're a genius," I said. "We can ask questions all day long, and no one will get suspicious. Tomorrow's Friday, and I got to cut the Feather sisters' grass, so I'll talk to them then."

"I'll take Burma," said Justice.

"I want to look for other typewriters too," I said. "That note could've been typed anywhere—not just at Gramps's house. But Lord only knows how I'm going to do that without looking obvious."

Liberty cleared her throat. "You realize *everyone* had typewriters back then, right? And the chance folks still have them is, like, practically nonexistent."

"I know, but I can't just sit around and do nothing, letting Gramps look guilty."

Mama's voice floated upstairs as the front door closed. I put my finger to my lips, signaling Justice and Liberty to be quiet. From the lilt of her tone, she was asking a question, and even though I couldn't make out her words, I recognized the low grumbling voice that answered her.

"It's Beau!" I slammed the closet doors shut. "I don't want him seeing our notes or anything. I need that like a snakebite."

"Coop!" Mama called from downstairs. "Our guest is here."

Which, loosely translated, meant *your living nightmare is about to begin.*

"I'm coming." I took a deep breath and turned to Justice and Liberty. "Act natural."

Liberty leaned against the closet doors and tossed her baseball back and forth between her hands. Justice flopped on my bed with a book from my nightstand.

"Justice, I said act *natural.*" I grabbed the book from his hand and wandered out to the landing. At the bottom of the steps, Beau stood between Mama and Tick holding a duffel bag. Mama looked up at me. She arched her brow, saying nothing, but still managing to get her point across. It was a warning shot.

"Head upstairs, Beau, dear," Mama said. "You must be exhausted. Coop will show you where you're sleeping. Just make yourself at home." She smiled sweetly at him, but it was wasted. He never bothered to look up from the floor. He dragged himself up the steps, clomping as he went. You'd think he wore cement blocks instead of dirty running shoes.

It was the first time I'd seen Beau since our fight. The colors on and around his nose matched those on and around my eye. I turned away as he reached the top step and stalked into my room.

"You're over there," I said, not even bothering to point to the made-up mattress in the corner. He could figure it out.

Beau threw his overnight bag onto the floral comforter. It bounced off and rolled onto the floor. "Only reason I'm here is 'cause your house is closer to the hospital."

"*I* don't want you here any more than you want to be here." I joined Liberty and leaned against the closet door, crossing my arms.

Glaring, he sat on the bed, pressed his back against the wall, and drew his knees up. He looked like a cornered animal.

Liberty's eyes darted over to Beau as she caught her ball. "Sorry about your dad, Beau."

He grunted. "What are you losers doing here?"

Liberty's jaw tightened.

"They're not losers," I shot back.

Justice swung his legs off my bed and walked around to where Beau sat. "She was just being nice. The only loser here is—"

Tick tapped on the door and walked in. "All settled, Beau?"

He nodded.

Tick reached into his pocket and handed Beau a slip of paper. "Here's the number to the hospital and your dad's doctor. He said call whenever you want. And Coop's mom said she'll drive you up to see your dad tomorrow."

Beau took the paper.

Tick turned and eyed me with a look I swear Mama had taught him. "Good night, Coop." He nodded at the twins. "Justice. Liberty."

At night I'd usually lay in bed, face the window, and stare at the moon. Then I'd replay memories of Daddy like an old movie reel in my head. When he was alive, he and I often stayed up late on full-moon nights and see who could spot the Man in the Moon first. Since his death, full moons had become, well…sacred.

Beau ruined that. He slept next to the window.

I didn't want him anywhere near my line of sight, so I rolled over and stared at the closet doors. But there were no memories of Daddy on those doors. I didn't care about Gramps's rule about not leaving a bad situation without finding two good things about it. There was nothing good about Beau being here, and he couldn't leave soon enough.

CHAPTER 24

I WOKE UP EARLY AND crept downstairs for breakfast. For all I knew, Mama was going to force Beau and me to eat every meal together, and I was not about to let that happen. I dropped the last Pop-Tart in the toaster with a smile. Beau would be stuck with plain ol' cereal.

Mama appeared in the doorway just as the toaster spit out my pastry. "Is Beau still asleep?"

I couldn't care less and shrugged. "Guess so."

She shuffled toward the coffee pot and tapped the brew button. "I'm not going to preach at you, but I hope you understand Beau didn't somehow orchestrate all this just so he could make your life miserable. He isn't happy, either."

"I know. But I hope no one here thinks we're suddenly going to become friends just because he's staying here. He can ignore me, I'll ignore him."

"Your dad had to learn to get along with people he didn't necessarily like in the Marines," she said.

"He was also trained to take out an enemy without leaving a mark."

Mama put her hand on her hip. "Cooper."

I put my hands up. "Sorry."

"All I'm saying is, it might be hard to cold-shoulder someone you're sharing a room with and who's walking alongside you to school every day. Make an effort, okay?"

"I seriously doubt Beau will walk alongside me," I muttered.

~~~

I was right. Beau trudged behind Liberty, Justice, and me when we walked to school that Friday morning. As we hurried to Miss Grupe's classroom, it occurred to me there was a lot of pointing and whispering in my direction. I chose to believe it was because everyone knew Beau was staying at my house.

The other option was people thought my gramps murdered his wife.

Miss Grupe was cool and didn't make a big deal about my return. Right before the end of the school day, she tapped her podium with her ruler. "Before you're dismissed, I want to discuss our first essay of the year. The theme is 'time.'"

She dismissed our protests with a wave of her hand. "I made

it a broad theme on purpose. You can research a specific event in time or explore how our society has changed over time. And so on. I'll give you a few minutes to brainstorm ideas with each other. Then I'll come around and write down the topic you've chosen."

Liberty scooted her desk up to mine. "Change in technology," she said. "That's what you can do."

Beau leaned across the aisle. "Bo—ring," he said, butting into our conversation.

"No one asked you," I said.

Liberty ignored him. "That way you can hunt for typewriters without looking suspicious. Just visit everyone on the suspect list, tell them you're doing research and need to see how old typewriters work—provided they still have one. Type a few sentences and then you'll have samples to compare to the goodbye letter."

"Suspect list?" Beau sneered. "What are you dorks talking about?"

"Nothing," I said. "Lib, that's a great idea."

Justice tapped his fingers on his desk. "I'm going to do something about the Civil War. That's what I'm best at. If it ain't broke, don't fix it."

Beau stared out the window. "Whatever."

Miss Grupe stopped by and wrote down our topics. I didn't hear what Beau's topic was, and I didn't care.

~~~~~

"How long will this take?" Beau scuffed his feet along the sidewalk. "I want to see my dad."

To make my life even more miserable, earlier that morning Mama had said since it was lawn-mowing Friday, Beau and I had to go the Feather sisters' house *together* after school, because she didn't want Beau feeling neglected. She never even asked Beau, but twenty bucks says he would've jumped on the idea of being left alone.

I shrugged. "An hour? It's not a big yard. Anyway, I'm sure your dad's still out cold. Tick would've said if he wasn't."

"I still want to see him, *Doctor Cooper*." He switched to kicking loose gravel when we turned into the driveway. "Why do you call him Tick? It's dumb."

My friendship with Tick, no matter how strained it was at the moment, was none of his business.

"Look." I jerked to a stop in the driveway. "It's pretty obvious the adults got together and came up with a stupid plan." I finger-quoted "plan." "They must think if they force us to hang out, that we'll stop fighting."

Beau crossed his arms. "We won't."

That was the first thing we'd *ever* agreed on in our lives.

"But if they think it's working, maybe they'll stop."

He turned to me. "Fine," he said through a clenched jaw.

He followed me around to the back, then peered into the shed when I slid the rusted door open.

"That piece of junk is their lawn mower?"

"It looks worse in the light." I pushed Ol' Feisty out the door.

"*Humph.*" He stepped inside to poke around, leaving me to wonder if that was an attempt at a laugh.

"Cooooop!" Miss Ruth called from the back stoop of the house. "Come inside and join an old lady for a ham-and-mustard sandwich. I just got a new jar in from Argentina."

Beau walked out from the shadow of the shed.

"Oh!" Miss Ruth perked up. "You've got a friend with you today."

Beau made a sound somewhere between a snort and a choke.

"Oh goodness me, you're Angus's boy, aren't you? Hello, Beau, dear. So glad to see you two getting on. You come in too."

"We're not getting on," muttered Beau.

"Argentina, huh?" I said, leaving Ol' Feisty near the shed. "Extra spicy?"

She looked over her shoulder and grinned. "Might melt your ears clean off."

Every Friday since I first started cutting their grass, she'd been inviting me in for ham-and-mustard sandwiches. Said she wanted to put more meat on my bones, but truthfully some of her mustards sweated *off* more meat than they ever put on.

Beau clomped up the steps after us.

We followed her down the hallway that begged for a fresh coat of paint. Tucked into an alcove stood a hat rack disguised as a large exotic bird due to the ridiculous number of feathered hats that perched on its wooden arms. A vase of fresh-cut flowers from the sisters' small front garden bed sat near the kitchen sink. Miss Ruth's collection of used mustard jars, now filled with a rainbow of colored marbles, sat on the windowsill, twinkling in the sunlight. She had enough to fill each sill in the kitchen.

Mustard was cheaper than traveling on a teacher's pension, so whenever she got a hankering to travel, she'd order spicy mustard from a faraway place instead. And if she wasn't buying them, she was making them. Over the years she and I had both tortured and treated our mouths to some pretty potent flavors.

"Where's Miss Meriwether today?" I asked as she handed each of us a ham-and-mustard on white.

"Suds was headed up to Piggly Wiggly and offered to give her a ride."

Miss Ruth and Miss Meriwether had never learned to drive, mainly 'cause they never owned a car. Said that was too expensive too. They walked everywhere or hitched rides when they could.

She poured a couple glasses of cold milk and set them on table. "And here's your extinguishers in case you find yourself 'bout to catch fire."

"Thanks." I stood, waiting for her to sit before I joined her at the table. Mama was stricter than a diet when it came to manners.

Beau held his sandwich plate with both hands, looking nervous. For someone who couldn't even manage to get along with regular kids his own age, having a snack with eccentric Miss Ruth was probably a nightmare.

"I don't bite, dear. I leave that to the mustard." She chuckled and smoothed her dress under her as she lowered herself into a chair.

He hesitated, but then sat.

"Coop and I have been doing this for a long time, haven't we, sugar?"

"Yes ma'am. And 'fore me, I guess you and my gran used to have yourselves some ham-and-mustard too."

Miss Ruth's face lit up in surprise.

"I read that bit in her journal." I bit off a large chunk of sandwich. In hindsight, it was a poor decision. The mustard set my throat on fire and then whooshed into my nostrils.

Miss Ruth nodded her head with a grin. "Tabby and I shared many wonderful moments with mustard." She giggled. "She was such a good sport about trying new flavors. She was the one who suggested I add rosemary to one of my recipes. And wouldn't you know—I won first place at that year's Pioneers Days Festival thanks to her." She patted her curls. "I had my picture made in the newspaper."

A human sparkler. That's what I felt like as heat moved from the back of my throat, up the sides of my skull, and then escaped out through my hair, shooting sparks off in different directions.

"That's Mama's favorite," I squeaked. "Mine too. And Mama doesn't even like rosemary, but she *loves* what you gave us for Christmas last year."

She smiled, but her eyes hinted at sorrow. "I miss Tabby. Aside from Meriwether, she was my best friend."

Beads of sweat had broken out on Beau's forehead, and I think his eyes watered more than mine. A tinge of pink crept up his neck but morphed to fire-engine red above his eyebrows.

Miss Ruth sat up in her chair, ignoring the flames shooting from my ears. "An idea has popped into my head that's, well, practically next to brilliant." She faced Beau. "I just happen to have your mama's old school map in my attic! Did you know she was a teacher? It used to be mine, but I gave it to her during her first year at Windy Bottom. When she died, I hung it back in my classroom as a way to remember her."

Miss Ruth, oblivious to our near combustion, continued. "I say we bring it down and look up every country we've tasted. Then Beau, pumpkin, you can take it home. What do you think?"

A trickle of sweat ran down my back. My tongue was swollen and prickly. It was a come-to-Jesus mustard if ever there was one.

I grabbed my milk. "You need us"—*chug, chug, gulp*—"to go up to your attic"—chug, gulp—"and look for a map?"

Beau mopped his forehead with his napkin and reached for his milk. "Wow," he squeaked.

Miss Ruth grinned. "Habanero chilies—that's what gives it its zing." She picked up the jar and showed us. "Tres Fuegos Mustard."

I nodded and wiped away a new trickle of sweat running down my face. "That's probably the strongest one yet."

"Meriwether can't stand the stuff, but we love it, don't we, Coop?" Miss Ruth smiled and stood. "Let's go, boys. Meriwether will be home soon, and she's such a fussbudget about me going up to the attic." She grinned like a kid sneaking cookies from a jar. "So now's our chance. We've a map to find."

CHAPTER 25

WE FOLLOWED HER BACK DOWN the hall and up the stairs to the landing. She pointed to a rope cord hanging from the attic trapdoor in the ceiling and turned to me. "Go on, sugar, pull on that rope and bring the door down."

I lowered the door and unfolded the narrow ladder.

"You boys go up first. I'll be right behind you. A lady in a dress never climbs a ladder first."

Frankly, seeing Miss Ruth's knickers was something I *did not ever* want to experience. I glanced at Beau. His face was still pink, but whether that was because of the mustard or because he too had been spared from a potential full moon was unknown to me.

Two things struck me when I climbed inside the attic. The first was the late-summer heat. The second was the dust.

Grime on the small solitary window set in the far side of the attic kept most of the sunlight on the outside. Dust floated through the air, reminding me of the mist-filled mornings we'd have once the cooler breath of autumn came. The kind where you'd see the actual specks of moisture suspended in air—only in this case it was dirt.

"I believe there's a light switch just to your right." Miss Ruth's voice called up to me.

I flipped it on. "Found it."

The single bulb was about as useful as the *k* in Beau's last name for all the light it gave off. I pulled out my phone and used the flashlight.

If a junkyard and antique store were to get married, the Feather sisters' attic would be their love child. To my right was a furniture graveyard made up of broken armchairs, a crib, and a wooden coffee table covered with watermarks. An antique-looking pole lamp lay in three pieces alongside a scarred chest of drawers and random bed frame parts. A rocking chair sat in one corner; a porcelain doll slumped against its spindled back. Maybe hidden somewhere in the mess was a typewriter.

"Whoa, look at all this stuff." Beau's head popped through the attic opening. "Creepy." He pointed over my shoulder.

I shined my light where he'd pointed. A ventriloquist doll hung by its strings from one of the rafter nails.

I shuddered.

Miss Ruth cleared her throat. "A little assistance, please, boys."

Beau turned and helped her through the opening and to her feet. It wasn't a move I expected to see.

Miss Ruth patted his cheek when she stood at the top. "Thank you, dear." She turned her attention to the attic. "Our family's never been one to throw stuff out, and we've years of junk to prove it. Throw away an item, you throw away a memory. And you both know how precious memories can be." She looked at Beau with softened eyes. "You never know when you might lose someone dear to you."

Beau jutted his chin out. "My dad's gonna be fine."

Miss Ruth nodded. "The best doctor this town's ever had was there to help him."

Beau huffed. "He didn't help my mom."

She shook her head. "Doesn't mean he didn't try. And that begrudging weight you've been carrying won't help you grow any taller, either, dear. Now, where to start?" She turned to scan the attic and missed the drop of Beau's jaw.

I don't think she meant it as a jab. More like a statement of fact.

"Like I said," she continued, "I haven't been up here in ages. Meriwether's always been the one to come grab the decorations and such. Says the dust bothers my asthma too much. Such a tender creature, that one."

I swiped at a cobweb. "How big is the map, Miss Ruth?"

She furrowed her brow. "It's a good size."

Whatever that meant.

"I'll start over in this corner." I climbed over a broken armchair and collided with a hat rack. I caught it before it crushed several dusty artificial poinsettia arrangements. It was cumbersome climbing around with one hand grasping my phone, but I wanted to be ready to take a photo for the case closet if I came across a typewriter. I was going to document everything just the way a real detective would.

Miss Ruth sneezed.

"Bless you," said Beau, before I could.

That was the first time I'd ever heard him say something polite. Either the mustard had sweated some meanness out of Beau, or some of Miss Ruth's character was rubbing off on him.

Miss Ruth and I sifted through trunks, boxes, and crates. We peered behind furniture and faded artwork and swiped at more cobwebs than at last year's haunted house. Beau was on the opposite side of the attic.

"Miss Ruth," I glanced behind the hundredth old milk crate stuffed with vinyl records, "do you have a typewriter?"

She popped out from behind a floor-length mirror with a floor-length crack. "What on earth do you want an old dinosaur like that for?"

"For school. I got to write an essay on changes in technology." I said it real official like so she wouldn't be skeptical. "I'd love to see how a typewriter works, and I thought I'd ask since we're up here."

"I used to have a typewriter back when I taught, but not anymore. Can't rightly remember what happened to it."

My heart sank.

She hummed as she continued searching. Miss Ruth was so nice. I was sorry Gramps had hurt her all those years back—broken his promise. On the other hand, I never would've been born if he'd married Miss Ruth instead of Tabby. I looked over my shoulder. Beau was busy at the far end.

"Miss Ruth?" I hesitated.

"Yes." Her voice came from behind a dress mannequin.

I bit my lip. Maybe she didn't want me to know about her and Gramps. What if I was about to embarrass her? Could she still be upset by what had happened all those years ago? It was hard to know what memories she held on to. She looked at me expectantly. I mentally kicked myself for having opened my mouth.

"It's just…" I swallowed and took a deep breath. "I heard about you and Gramps. How y'all used to be…you know… together." Now I just wanted to get it over with. "I'm sorry things didn't work out. I love my Gramps, but I don't think it was right that he didn't keep his promise to you."

"Oh, Coop, dear." She smiled and crossed the floor to me. "I forgave him. It was understandable, your grandmother being an heiress and such. I suppose the temptation was just too—"

"Wait." I frowned. "A what?"

"An heiress, dear. With an enormous trust fund."

"An heiress?" A pit formed in my stomach. "I knew she had money but I—I didn't know *that*. I just thought…" The words crept out in a whisper. Gramps said she was wealthy, but an heiress somehow sounded way richer than just "wealthy."

Where is the money now?

Her fingers flew to her lips. "Oh dear. Maybe I shouldn't have said anything." Her voice trailed off as she looked to the floor. She sighed, and let her hands fall to her side. "Oh well, too late now—cat's out of the bag. I suppose the responsible thing to do is tell you *everything*, so at least you have the facts."

Whether or not I'd be getting facts from Miss Ruth was anybody's guess.

She knelt and rifled through a steamer trunk that had probably been on the *Titanic*, it was in such rough shape. "Rumor had it her folks died in a car accident, leaving her with more money than sense." Her eyes darted to me. "I'm not saying she was dumb, sugar, only that youth and a large inheritance don't often go well together." She spoke soft and slow in her usual singsongy tone.

I looked once more over my shoulder toward Beau, then back to Miss Ruth. "How rich was she?"

She pulled out an ugly hat. "Oh, I make it a point *never* to talk about money. It's not polite. However," she leaned in, "a little bird told me her daddy was in the shipping business. Your gramps was never left wanting. But when they married, that whole 'what's mine is yours and yours is mine' thing came in handy, that much was for sure."

She looked at the hat in her hand. "Isn't this just awful looking? A red feather would go far in its improvement. Or maybe purple." She blew on beige felt, and a cloud of dust flew up. Dropping it on her head, she grinned in the mirror. "This is fun. Even if it is hot."

I didn't answer. When rich people die, suspects are everywhere. No one is excluded. Especially not Gramps. Where there's money, there's motive. I didn't think he married Tabby for her money. But some people might wonder. The pit in my stomach grew heavier. I changed the subject.

"Miss Ruth, the school newspaper wants to do an article on my grandma."

"That's nice. I didn't know the school had a paper."

"It's a recent thing," I said. "I'd love to interview you, since y'all were friends."

"Anything for you, Coop." She set the hat back in the trunk

and picked up an ugly pink lace fan. She stood, opened the fan, and waved it back and forth.

I wished I had a list of questions, but I didn't. "What do you remember about Tabby?"

She smiled and seemed to retreat into her memory. "I remember she always looked like a fashion model. Beautiful dress and hat anytime she left the house." She chuckled and touched her neck. "And I remember the way she always fiddled and fidgeted with the emerald necklace your grandfather bought her for their anniversary. She loved it. Fancy jewelry never looked out of place on Tabby."

Beau tripped over a rolled-up rug and let out a curse.

"Language, dear," Miss Ruth called over her shoulder.

"Were you surprised to hear she'd run off?" I moved a box out of my way.

With a flick of her wrist she whipped the fan shut. "Honey bee, Tabby moving from Atlanta to Windy Bottom was like putting a show horse in a mule barn. So much class and no place to parade it. Your grandfather called me the night she left and read me her goodbye note. I was shocked she left her baby, but I knew she missed the big city something fierce. Poor little Steven. Only a year old." She *tsk-tsked*. "Of course, *now* we know that's not what happened."

"Do you remember the day she left?" I cleared my throat. "I mean, died."

Miss Ruth chuckled and reached out to smack my leg with the fan. "Cooper Goodman, are you asking me if I had an alibi?"

"Oh no, ma'am!" I stuttered. Heat rushed to my face. "I—I was just, uh—uh I wondered because I thought—"

"Relax, dearie. I'm just teasing you." She grinned. "Being a teacher, I would've been up at the school all day attempting to pour knowledge into my students' heads. A worthless cause on some days, I'll tell you that."

Duh. She hadn't always been retired.

"Over here," said Beau, climbing over a trunk.

Leaning in the corner, almost hidden by a rack of old winter coats and other garments, was a rolled-up map.

He stretched. "Got it." He turned and held the map victoriously.

"Wonderful!" Miss Ruth clapped.

Beau wiggled his way out from behind the boxes and handed the giant roll to Miss Ruth.

"Hold that end, dear, there's something I want to show you." She took the other end and slowly stepped away, unrolling the map. She stopped. "There, see that?" She pointed near the bottom. *To Cordelia—Welcome to Windy Bottom High. Have a great year. Ruth Feather.* "She taught geography and history just like me." She turned to me. "Coop, darlin', take a picture of Beau with the map. That way he can take a copy to the hospital when he visits his daddy." She smiled at Beau. "You can tell him all about it. People can hear you even when they're in a coma. That will make him feel better—I just know it."

I pulled my phone from my pocket and took a photo.

"Get the inscription too, dear. Beau can read it to his daddy. Maybe even just hearing the name of his poor dead wife will help him." Miss Ruth sighed. "We never know what brings people back, do we?"

Beau looked like he wasn't sure what to say. I moved between him and Miss Ruth and photographed the inscription.

"Excellent." She walked back toward Beau, letting the map roll up.

It was taller than Beau, and he leaned on it like a shepherd's staff. "Thanks, Miss Ruth." He scuffed his shoe back and forth across the attic floor. "Dad won't talk about her, and I don't have anything of hers. I really—"

"What in blue blazes is going on up here?" Miss Meriwether's head popped through the attic door opening, her face pinched in a scowl.

Beau froze. I don't know what look Miss Meriwether shot at him, but the expression on his face made him look like a total chicken. Nothing instilled fear faster than being on the crabby end of Miss Meriwether.

"Y'all have stirred up more dust than a black blizzard!" She joined us at the top, coughing and waving her hand. "Ruth, get down before your asthma kicks in."

"Oh, Meriwether," Miss Ruth chided. "Be nice to the boys. They were helping me find Cordelia's old school map," she said dismissively. "Now step aside, so I can use the ladder." She grabbed the rails with both hands and eased herself down the steps. "Bring the map with you, dears," she sang.

Ruth's voice trailed as she and Meriwether walked away, "...such a mother hen, Meriwether...we're going to look...the different countries...mustard...Beau should keep it..."

Beau, map in hand, went down first.

I skipped the last couple steps and jumped down, then folded the ladder and let the springs swallow the door back up into the ceiling.

When I turned, there was Beau. "You waited?"

Beau shook his head. "I sure as heck wasn't going to go down there by myself."

"Guess I can't blame you." I muttered as I turned and headed down the stairs. "Come on, I still got to cut their grass."

Miss Ruth's revelation in the attic about Tabby's inheritance was a bombshell that left my brain churning with questions, and even the challenge of steering Ol' Feisty around the flower beds didn't distract me. What *did* Gramps do with all the money after she left? Did people in town think he'd married her for it? Did the police know how much she'd had? Officers Harrison and Watkins had carried boxes from Gramps's office. Maybe they were crammed full of financial stuff. With each piece of information I found, more questions came.

CHAPTER 26

I FINISHED AND COLLECTED MY five dollars from Miss Ruth. Beau and I grabbed our backpacks from the porch and headed home.

He carried the map in his hand and kicked stones down the sidewalk. "I'm not about to play detective with you idiots, and it was nice of Miss Ruth to give me this map, but it sounded to me like she didn't like Tabby much, the way she talked about her being kind of stupid and all. And that whole 'we were best friends and I forgave your grandfather' speech? Totally bogus."

"What are you talking about?" I was hot and grimy from cutting the grass, and the fifty pounds of books in my school bag was making my shirt stick to my body. I wanted to wipe the smirk off Beau's smug face…with my backpack. "Gran even wrote in her journal they were friends. You don't know anything."

He stopped walking. "How dumb are you?" He looked at me and shook his head. "I know snark when I hear it. Just listen to my dad."

When we walked through the front door, voices were traveling from the kitchen. I recognized Deputy Gomez's as it mixed in with Mama and Gramps's.

"verify if this...emerald necklace?" Gomez was saying.

Emerald necklace? I turned to Beau and put my finger to my lips. He rolled his eyes and jogged upstairs. I scurried down the hall, ducked into the bathroom next to the kitchen, then peered around the doorway. The three of them were leaning over the kitchen table looking at something and blocking my view.

"Found in a pawnshop in Sangerville," continued Gomez. "Some guy named Lear Stowinn—two n's—hocked it there a couple days ago...pretty suspicious timing if you ask me."

Lear Stowinn? Who the heck is Lear Stowinn?

"Two days ago? That was Wednesday," Mama said with surprise.

Gramps's brow furrowed. "Lear Stowinn, you say? Never heard of him."

Deputy Gomez straightened up from the table. "That's because he doesn't exist. Name's a fake."

"So you don't know who he really is?" Mama's voice sagged with disappointment. "But surely the shopkeeper can describe

COOP KNOWS THE SCOOP

him. Or security cameras? It could help Harley if someone's on camera selling the necklace of his murdered wife." She looked to Gramps. "Sorry if that sounds crass, Harley."

Gramps shrugged. "It's the truth, though."

Gomez crossed his arms. "Unfortunately, the guy seemed to know where the cameras were. He kept his head down and his body turned away. All we know is it was an older man"—he turned to Gramps—"about your height and weight. Where were *you* Wednesday?"

"Here we go again," muttered Gramps. "I was here all afternoon and evening."

"And I'll vouch for him," said Mama, shooting poison darts at Gomez with her eyes.

"What about in the morning?" The eye darts bounced off Deputy Gomez's chest.

Gramps fiddled with his watch. A sure sign he was nervous. "I went for a drive. Had to clear my head."

"You alone?"

The question hung in the air before Gramps answered with a nod.

"Where did you drive?"

"Just around."

"Sangerville?"

"No," Gramps said through a clenched jaw. "Why would I

tell the police the necklace was missing and then turn around and pawn it? That doesn't even make sense."

"It doesn't make sense for *anyone* to hock it all these years later, but someone did. Right now I'm asking *you* about it," said Deputy Gomez.

"Give me a break," said Gramps.

"Maybe the financial need wasn't as great back then. Lawyers can be expensive, and you clearly need one now." Deputy Gomez paused, then picked up a photo from the table and his hat. "We'll be in touch. No more long drives in the country, Dr. Goodman, if you don't mind. Not until we get this solved." He looked to Mama and nodded. "Ma'am. I'll see myself out."

"I want the necklace back when you're done," Gramps hollered down the hall.

He sank into a kitchen chair. Mama put her hand on his shoulder. "It'll be okay, Harley. You'll see."

Those were the exact words she'd told me when Gramps was taken away for questioning a couple days ago. I was beginning to wonder how many times they'd be spoken.

Thanks to the fact Mama had taken Beau up to the hospital to see Angus—even though his condition hadn't changed—I had my room all to myself. I opened my closet doors and pulled down the

question list. *Who is Lear Stowinn and how did he get Gran's necklace?*
Then I checked to see if I could answer any of them. Only a few.

1. Who wrote the goodbye note? Tabby?

2. Where is Tabby's emerald necklace?—at the police station (pawned by Lear Stowinn)

3. How did she die?—arsenic (rat poison?)

4. ✶✶✶Who killed her and why?✶✶✶

5. Is Gramps a suspect?—yes

6. Where is Earl? Did he steal the necklace?—Who knows and no

7. Who was stealing from the church's memorial fund? The bookkeeper?

8. Who was the bookkeeper at Windy Bottom Baptist 40 years ago?

I stopped and checked my email to see if Pastor Joel had responded with the answer to #8. Nothing.

9. Did Gran's death have anything to do with the stolen money?

10. What happened to Gran's inheritance?

11. Who is Lear Stowinn?

12. How did he get the emerald necklace?

I made a suspect card for Lear Stowinn and added it to the suspect wall. Too bad there was no photo. Then I added a couple notes to the Feather sisters' cards of things I'd learned while at their house:

—Miss Ruth often made ham-and-mustard sandwiches for Tabby.
—Miss Ruth said Tabby was an heiress to a shipping fortune.
—Miss Meriwether was mad we were in the attic. She shooed us out right quick. Is she hiding something?

Man! I puffed out my cheeks. I thought I had a lot of questions a couple days ago. Now I had too many questions, too many suspects, and no help. At least tomorrow was Saturday, and it wouldn't matter if I was grounded. Liberty, Justice, and I worked at the bookstore on Saturdays. I could talk to them then without worrying about Beau getting in my face about it.

CHAPTER 27

TEN MINUTES BEFORE A LATTÉ Books was set to open, Liberty
sauntered through the swinging kitchen door, tossing her baseball
back and forth in her hands. "What's Bo Peep doing here?" she
whispered to me.

I glanced over to History, where Beau shelved new books.

"I blame your mom," I grumbled as I wiped down the latté
machine.

"My mom?"

"Yeah, 'cause she's not here, we're a man short. Beau got
roped into helping." I tossed her a dishcloth. "Look busy. Mama's
in the storeroom but will be out here soon. Where's Justice?"

"The bathroom." She grimaced. "And he *won't* be here soon.
Dad's cooking isn't nearly as safe as Mama's."

While we waited for Justice, I told her about the police finding the emerald necklace, the mysterious Lear Stowinn, and how Deputy Gomez probably suspected Gramps of pawning the necklace for insurance money.

"I guess ol' Sticky Fingers Earl didn't take it, after all." She made a face and leaned on the counter. "Bet he still filched Chester's dog tag, though. And the police have no idea who this Lear Stowinn guy is?"

I shook my head, then told her what Miss Ruth had let slip in the attic about Gran's inheritance.

"Wait. Your grandma was loaded?" Liberty raised her brows. "No offense, Coop, your place is nice, but it doesn't exactly scream high cotton. Where'd all the money go?"

"I don't know." I walked around to the other side of the counter and checked the napkin supply. "I've been wondering that too. Maybe it's not true and was just a rumor. But Miss Ruth thinks it's true, which supports our theory of her wanting Gran out of the way. Maybe she thought if she got Gramps, she'd be rich."

Liberty frowned. "Actually, I *have* been thinking about that, and I'm pretty sure Miss Ruth needs to be nixed as a suspect."

I stopped. "What? Why?"

"Think about it. If Miss Ruth had killed Tabby so she could marry your gramps, why write a note to make it look like she ran off? Miss Ruth would *want* the body discovered so your gramps would know his wife was dead. That's the *only* way he'd be free to marry again."

I slapped my forehead with the palm of my hand. "Argh! You're right. That'd be dumb." But a good part of me was relieved. The thought of Miss Ruth as a suspect never sat right with me. "Plus, my gran might've been skinny, but she was tall, and the Feather sisters don't drive. No way could Miss Ruth have carried her all the way to the playground to bury her."

"But you have the same problem of figuring out how Miss Meriwether would've moved the body."

"Nah. Miss Meriwether's built like a Mack truck. She could've done it. Maybe she hid the body until it was dark, and then dragged her to the playground."

Liberty arched a brow. "Maybe." She grabbed a broom from the corner and came around to where I stood. "What I want to know is *why* the playground? It seems like a really creepy place to bury someone."

"I asked Gramps about that too. He said he remembers the playground had just been installed a couple days before Tabby had 'run off.' Maybe whoever killed her took advantage of that fact. You know how hard the dirt here is. It'd definitely be easier to dig a grave if the ground had just been broken up for playground equipment."

Justice sauntered in rubbing his stomach. "Hey Coop. FYI, Burma's no longer a suspect. He was in Texas the same week your gran was murdered. His exact words were 'I came back to the news about Tabby and a line of people wrapped around my shop just itching to chin-wag.' I'm thinking *chin-wag* means to gossip or something." Then he belched. "Excuse me."

"You sure he's telling the truth?"

Justice nodded. "He and his sister competed in a bowling tournament. They had their picture taken in front of the banner with the date on it. He wasn't here."

I made a mental note to throw Burma's suspect card away. "That helps narrow down the list of suspects, though—we're down to Earl Winston and Meriwether Feather."

"And Lear Stowinn," said Liberty.

"Who?" asked Justice.

She filled him in.

"Oh! Hey, guess what?" Justice slugged me in the arm. "I also found out Earl's got a typewriter."

"Really?"

"He's back? You *asked* him?" asked Liberty.

He shook his head. "I talked to Leroy after school. You can ask that guy anything when he's plunging a toilet. Last year he answered half my math questions after someone clogged the one in the teachers' lounge."

"Get to the point, Jus," Lib said.

"Leroy said Earl's too stingy to throw anything out. He's always hoping his junk will be valuable one day. Said Earl keeps everything stashed in the funeral home."

A spark of hope ignited. "I gotta find it and test it."

"You know Earl's not just going to let you mess around with his typewriter." Justice rubbed the back of his neck. "Especially if he *did* type the fake letter."

"We got to do something." I fixated on the floor, like the answer was there. "He has a typewriter, *and* his blood was found on Tabby's ring—we still don't know why."

"What do you suggest?" Lib licked her thumb and rubbed away a smear of dirt on her ball.

"I don't know."

"I'll tell you what you do." Beau poked his head around a bookshelf.

"Cripes, Beau!" Liberty jumped. "Didn't your daddy ever teach you it's rude to listen in on other people's conversations?"

He leaned against the shelf and crossed his feet. "Nope."

"What all did you hear?" I asked.

"Enough."

"Okay, then, what should we do?" asked Liberty.

"Easy." He shrugged. "Earl's not in town. You break into the funeral parlor, duh."

And that's the moment when Beau and I started getting along.

"I'm good with anagrams," he added.

"Good for you," Liberty said scowling. "Why do we care?"

"Because if you rearrange the letters in '*Lear Stowinn*' you get '*Earl Winston*.'"

Liberty thought for a moment and then cussed…again.

"Sure," muttered Justice. "If I spell something, I'm an idiot, but *Beau* rearranges a few letters and everyone thinks he's a genius."

Beau leaned in Justice's face. "Check my IQ scores. I *am* a genius."

CHAPTER 28

THE SUN HAD LONG SINCE dipped below the horizon when Justice, Liberty, Beau, and I gathered in the living room for Operation Walking Dead.

"Please, Mama," I begged.

"We just want to walk around the square." Liberty clasped her hands and pleaded.

Justice nodded. "And we'll take flashlights just to be extra safe."

"The fresh air *would be* nice after seeing Dad," said Beau. "Hospitals smell kinda funny."

"Oh, Beau." Mama reached and gave his shoulder a gentle squeeze. "I understand." She looked to Gramps. "What do you think, Harley?"

Gramps folded down his paper from where he sat reading it

in his recliner. "For the love of Pete, Delilah, the four of them are actually getting along. Let them go. What kind of trouble do you think they're going to get into?"

"Thanks, Gramps!"

"No more than an hour, you hear?" called Mama.

"Yes, ma'am."

Gramps muttered something unintelligible and turned his focus back to his newspaper.

~~~

The closest I'd ever come to breaking the law was helping myself to the occasional cookie from the jar Mama kept hidden behind the pickled okra. Breaking into Earl's funeral parlor after sundown was definitely a step up.

We ducked into the empty back alley of Comforted Souls and gathered behind the rusted dumpster.

"Do you think he has a burglar alarm?" I asked.

"Doubt it," said Liberty. "What's a person to steal? A body?"

Beau shook his head. "He doesn't have one."

All three of us stared at him. I was better off not knowing too much about Beau's techniques. I glanced at my watch. Mama had given us only an hour. "We're running out of time."

Beau poked his head around the side of the dumpster and shined his flashlight on the back door of the funeral parlor. "See the small window high in the wall to the left of the door? I think I can squeeze through."

"How you going to reach it?" I asked.

He shined his flashlight in my eyes. "You're going to give me a leg up, moron."

"Then what?" asked Justice.

Lib rolled her eyes. "He'll crawl through, unlock the back door, and let us in."

Beau peeked around the dumpster once more and then to Liberty and Justice. "Hey—Tweedledumb and Tweedledumber—go make sure no one's coming at either end of the street. Don't use a flashlight unless you have to. It draws attention. We'll wait here until y'all get back."

Liberty looked like she wanted to pick Beau up and toss him in the dumpster.

I looked at my watch again. "Hurry."

She and Justice scurried off in opposite directions.

Something had been poking at my brain ever since Beau butted into our conversation at the café that morning.

"Why are you helping, Beau?"

He jammed his hands into his pockets. "What else am I going to do on a Friday night with you losers?"

Then, as if he'd read my mind, he said, "And don't go figuring we're friends. 'Cause we're not."

Fair enough.

Liberty dashed behind the dumpster, and Justice followed a few moments later.

"We clear?" asked Beau.

"Yep," said Justice.

Liberty nodded. "Good to go."

"Follow me." Beau hurried to the back door of Comforted Souls. A dim light hung above the gray metal door. Beau pointed to Justice and then up to the light. "You're the tallest. Unscrew the bulb."

Beau used the hand railing near the door as a ladder. A moment later, we stood in darkness.

Beau faced me. "Okay, give me a leg up."

I crouched down and interlaced my fingers to create a stirrup. Beau placed a foot into my hands and reached for the window ledge.

He looked down. "Get me higher."

I slowly stood. My shoulders strained under his weight. "Sheesh, man, how many slices of pizza did you eat tonight?"

"Six. Why?"

I groaned as gravel from his shoes bit into my palm. "No reason."

"Almost there," Beau rasped.

And then suddenly the weight was gone. I looked up to see him slip through the window.

Lib fiddled with her ponytail. "Got to hand it to him. Who

eats six slices of pizza and still manages to squirm through a small window?"

The back door clicked open and Beau's face appeared. "Quick."

We flipped our flashlights on and scanned the area around us.

"Whoa," Liberty breathed. "Coffin central."

"It can't get any creepier than this." Justice's voice came from behind me.

Rows of crookedly stacked coffins lined the wall closest to us. More coffins rested on the other side of the wall too. Some were closed, others opened. Different styles, wood colors, and fabrics.

Justice came and stood next to me. "Do you think there's people inside the shut ones?"

"I hope not," I said.

"I'm gonna check."

"No! No time. And besides, that's disrespectful."

"Dude," Justice said. "We just broke into a funeral home. We passed *disrespectful* miles back." He rubbed his hand over the top of one. "Can't believe Earl got stuck in one of these things when he was a kid. That'll make anyone closetphobic."

"Claustrophobic," corrected Liberty.

"It's a storage area, I think." Beau shined his light across the coffins toward a hallway partially covered by a black velvet curtain. "That hall probably leads out front to the showroom. Maybe there's an office or something too."

"Are those urns?" Liberty elbowed me and shined her light on a shelf behind me holding several vases with lids.

"I think so." I shuddered. The idea someone's ashes could be sitting in them waiting for a family member to pick them up gave me chills.

Another doorway leading to a different room was on my left. I took a couple steps and looked inside, running my flashlight around the room. It sort of looked like a doctor's office, only bigger and weirder. A stainless steel table with a sink at one end stood in the middle. Shelves on the wall held different-sized bottles of colored fluids. A large red bin, with the word BIOWASTE stamped on the side, rested in the corner.

And the whole place smelled like our classroom last year when we dissected bullfrogs.

"It just got creepier," I said.

Liberty walked in and gasped. "The embalming room." She pointed her flashlight to a machine on the counter. It looked like a large watercooler only with hoses and tubes attached to the sides. "That's the thing that injects the embalming fluid into the bodies."

Beau focused on the machine. Even though we stood in near dark, I could tell his face had turned a kind of pasty gray. I wondered if the tubes coming from it reminded him of his daddy's hospital room. But we couldn't dwell. We needed to get moving.

"Let's split up and search," I said. "Beau and I'll take up

front, and, Jus, you and Lib take this place and the storeroom. And hurry. If we get caught, we're dead meat."

Justice grinned. "Then we're in the perfect place."

Liberty slugged him in the arm.

Beau kept staring at the machine. I pulled on his shirtsleeve. "Don't think about it, man. Come on."

We maneuvered our way through the maze of coffins. The clock on the wall ticked away the minutes in the otherwise silent room.

When we got to the velvet curtain, I pushed it aside and shined my flashlight down the hall. "You were right. The showroom is in front and"—I turned toward a door on my right—"this must be Earl's office. What a hoarder."

It was a small room, made even smaller by the ugly, oversized, floor-to-ceiling metal shelves covering the walls. Each one overflowed with all kinds of junk.

Beau turned in a circle, shining his light on the shelves. "There's more garbage here than what was in the Feather sisters' attic."

"Yeah. I just hope there's no ventriloquist doll hidden in all this stuff."

After several minutes of hunching over and searching, Beau stood and stretched. "Earl is one strange dude." He pointed to the shelf. "Look at this mess. He's got his business papers tossed in with these funky little Greek statues. Here're more urns—kinda disturbing having them in the same box as the salt and pepper shakers. Why do people collect salt and pepper shakers anyway? Same with little spoons or those thimble things. I don't get it."

"Beats me." I dug through a cardboard box on the bottom. Couldn't help but wonder if he was rambling 'cause maybe he was feeling nervous. I bet being at a funeral home while his daddy wasn't doing so hot at the hospital freaked him out. Truthfully, it freaked me out a bit too. Being surrounded by so many tools of death made me feel heavy and cold on the inside. Had Dad been in a place like this before his funeral? I hoped not.

Disheveled papers escaping from folders were stashed in old shoeboxes already filled with books, knickknacks, and really ugly garage-sale bargains. Mama would've loved it. Garage sales were her favorite.

"Do you think any of this stuff was stolen off dead people?"

Beau picked up a plate. "Unless someone croaked with this full set of china hidden in their pockets, I doubt it."

"Well, there's nothing on my end." I glanced at my watch again. "We're almost out of time."

"Hey!" Beau pointed the beam of light to the top shelf. "Is that it?"

I took a couple steps back to look. "Nah. That's an old cash register."

"No, next to the cash register but behind that small Chinese gong."

"Hold on." I grabbed Earl's chair from behind his desk and rolled it to the shelf, then climbed up. "Hold the chair." I stood on my toes, shined my flashlight toward the back, and craned my neck. "Yes!" I whisper-shouted. "You found it!" I moved the gong aside and held my flashlight with my teeth. I lifted the typewriter. It was heavier than I thought it would be. "Oh man," I garbled through my flashlight.

"Grow a muscle and hand it down," said Beau.

My arms strained as I lifted it over a mound of clutter on the shelf.

"*Achoo!*"

Beau's arms jerked with his sneeze. The chair jolted. My flashlight flew out of my mouth. I crashed into the giant shelf as the weight of the typewriter threw me off balance. I somewhat jumped but mostly fell to the floor...along with what felt like half the junk on the shelves. An avalanche of papers, books, and everything else crashed to the floor.

"Smooth move." Beau wrenched the typewriter from my gripping fingers and set it on Earl's cluttered desk. "Justice. Liberty," he called. "I found it."

"We heard," said Liberty, appearing in the doorway. "Along with the rest of the town." She began to pick up the items from the floor. "Give me a hand, Jus."

I picked myself off the floor and pulled a folded sheet of

paper from my back pocket I'd shoved in earlier. "I'll type a sentence. Hold your flashlight higher so I can see what I'm doing."

I tried to feed the paper through the roller, but my hands shook. My ribs struggled to contain the pounding of my heart. I stepped back, took a deep breath, and tried again.

"Here goes nothing," I said, pressing down the keys.

"Well?" Lib whispered.

I leaned over to examine the paper. "Nothing. As in there's *nothing* here. The ribbon must be dried out."

Not fair. All the sneaking and searching and we had zilch to show for it. We all stared at it. I don't know why. Maybe we hoped it would suddenly start working.

"Sorry, dude." Justice squeezed my shoulder. "You could still ask Tick to test it…maybe?"

I nodded. "Yeah. Maybe." I ran my hands through my hair and looked around. "Earl can't know we were here. We need to get this back where it was." I climbed back on the chair. "Hand it up to me."

I grabbed the typewriter from Justice while Beau held the flashlight toward the shelves. But what I saw in the beam of light almost made me drop it again.

"Hold on a minute, Justice. Take this back. Beau, keep your light there."

My breath caught in my throat. When I fell against the shelf I must've jostled some junk loose, because what I saw now wasn't there before. Mixed in with dust-covered teacups and dented cardboard boxes was a suitcase.

"Holy crap," I reached for the handle.

"What is that?" asked Beau.

I jumped off the chair. "Tabby's suitcase." I swallowed. Words didn't want to form. "I recognize it from the photos."

"You sure?" asked Liberty.

"Positive. It has her initials." I set it on top of the scattered papers on Earl's desk and flicked the metal latches open.

A handful of dresses and couple pairs of shoes. That was it. Gran's favorite orange-and-white striped dress by that designer dude wasn't there, though. If the dress wasn't here, and wasn't in the attic with the rest of her things…then where was it?

Liberty swore. "He must have killed your grandma and then faked everything to make it look like she ran off."

"There's the proof you wanted, Coop," said Justice.

"And took her necklace," said Beau. "I still think Earl and Lear are the same guy."

I felt the blood drain from my face. We were standing in the office of a murderer. What other explanation was there? It would be an open-and-shut case—as the cops on TV would say.

Justice shook his head in disgust. "For a guy who buries people for a living, you'd think he'd have known to dig the hole a little deeper."

Beau shrugged. "Maybe Earl was in a hurry. People don't think straight when they're rushed."

"We got to put all this back and call Deputy Gomez," I said.

"Why not Vidler? He's nicer," said Liberty.

"Tick isn't on the case anymore," I reminded her. "It doesn't matter the typewriter was a total bust. When we show this suitcase to Gomez, he'll arrest Earl—once they find him." I glanced at the wall clock. "We've got to hurry. We're out of time."

Liberty checked her watch. "Let's hope Deputy Gomez will listen to us and come quickly."

Her words got me thinking. What *if* Deputy Gomez didn't come to Earl's right away? Tick probably would've, but I didn't know Gomez well. Liberty had a point. Maybe it wasn't smart to leave the suitcase behind.

"Good point." I grabbed it. "We'll show Deputy Gomez and tell him where we found it. Put everything else back. Earl can't know we've been here."

With all the junk that had fallen from the shelves, it took us longer than I'd hoped to clean up.

"Now let's get out of here," I said.

I couldn't wait to get home. We had real evidence against Earl, and I could prove Gramps hadn't killed Tabby. I yanked open the back door.

The police car searchlight pointed right at our faces.

CHAPTER 29

"I'VE CALLED YOUR PARENTS, AND they should be here soon."
Tick stared at us as we stood with our backs against his police car.
He held Tabby's suitcase in his hand.

Several yards away, Earl stood at the back door, speaking with Deputy Gomez. A dingy gray bathrobe hung on his thin frame. His striped pajama bottoms almost covered up the fact he wore slippers.

Tick's eyes met mine. They seemed heavy, but not from lack of sleep. "What were you thinking?" He didn't wait for answer. He placed the suitcase on his car trunk and walked away.

I hadn't expected his words to hurt...but they did.

At least Tick hadn't cuffed us, and I knew once Mama arrived I'd be grounded (again), impounded, imprisoned, *plus* any other punishment that was considered legal, or possibly even illegal.

"How was I to know Earl'd come back?" I muttered. "And from visiting his mom of all things. He wasn't even on the run." I kicked the gravel.

Beau snorted. "If *somebody* hadn't fallen, it wouldn't have mattered."

I groaned. "If *somebody* hadn't sneezed, I wouldn't have fallen."

He squared his shoulders. "You think I did it on purpose? Even if I did, what are you going to do about it? Huh?" He pushed my shoulder.

I curled my fist. "How about a quick repeat of what happened in the library?"

Lib pulled me back, and Jus stepped in front of Beau.

"Coop!" Liberty said. "Beau didn't sneeze on purpose, and you know it."

Tick spun around. We all leaned back against the police car and examined our shoelaces.

"You've spent your whole life hating my Gramps." I forced the words out from my clenched jaw. "Why did you come anyway?"

Beau glared. "Because I owe your gramps one. And I don't like owing nobody, so I thought I'd pay up."

"You owe...? What are you talking about?"

"How stupid are you? Your gramps saved my dad's life. So,

duh, I owe your gramps." Beau took a deep breath. "And I wanted to help."

I met his stare, expecting to see the same anger in his eyes that I held in mine. But there was no anger. Just sincerity.

"I wish you two would make up your minds," muttered Liberty.

"Cooper Steven Goodman!" Mama's voice could've rearranged the night stars from where she stood next to her car in the alley. I felt all four of us try to shrink.

"What on earth were you thinking?" she said through her teeth.

I winced.

Why were adults always asking me that?

She stormed toward us with the ferociousness of a late-summer hurricane—the type that had enough strength to level a small town sitting a hundred miles inland.

Tick intercepted Hurricane Delilah before she got to us. He reached out and gently touched her shoulder and said something. If the words were "calm down," they had little impact. I wished he had put me *in* his car. At least then I'd be safe from Mama's rage.

"Just be glad your grandfather was already asleep when Keith called," she said glaring at me over Tick's shoulder.

I glanced at Lib, Jus, and Beau. They studied their shoes… again. Mr. Gordon had arrived the same as Mama but had yet to say anything, which was worse than actually saying *something*. He just glowered at the four of us.

"I thought you'd be proud, Mama," I choked.

Tick, Mama, and Mr. Gordon glanced wide-eyed at each other and then at me.

"Proud?" they repeated together.

Mama put her hands on her hip. "And why, pray tell, would I be proud to have the police call and tell me you were caught breaking into a funeral parlor?"

"Because I think—"

"Wrong!" Mama's hands slammed against hips. "The one thing you *didn't* do was think!"

Her voice echoed in the empty alley. Earl and Deputy Gomez both looked up from where they stood by the back door. Earl sneered.

"I am so disappointed in you," she said.

She probably thought if Daddy was still alive I wouldn't have done something so stupid.

I'd like to think if Daddy was still alive, he'd have taught me how to not get caught.

"But, Mama, we found—"

"I. Don't. Care." Mama seethed. "I don't care if you found the Holy Grail or the Lost City of Atlantis. You were breaking and entering!"

"—Tabby's murderer," I said.

She pressed both hands to her face and took a deep breath. She stared at Tick. "He's not listening. I can't. I can't even…" she turned away, her hands in the air.

"Tick," I pleaded. "We just wanted to test Earl's typewriter."

"Why?"

"To see if it matched Gran's goodbye letter."

Tick sighed. "I could have the four of you arrested, you realize that, right?"

"No, Keith, please." Mama turned and grabbed his arm.

"It's not up to me, Delilah." He gestured behind him to Earl. "If Earl wants to press charges, it's within his legal rights to do so."

"Do y'all know how much trouble you're in?" Mr. Gordon said.

I bit my lip. I hadn't actually thought we might end up in jail.

"But, Tick, the suitcase." I gestured to his car. "That was Gran's."

Mama looked where I pointed and gasped.

I pointed across the alley at Earl. "He had it. He must've killed Gran!"

Tick ran his hand over his face. "You'd better be careful of any accusations you make, Cooper." He walked over to the suitcase. "Where exactly did you find this?"

"Hidden in his office."

He rolled his eyes. "Great. Now Earl can add larceny to the list of charges. I hope you didn't take anything else." Tick turned to Mama. "You recognize this, Delilah?"

She nodded. "From pictures. Harley would know for sure, though."

"It was Gran's," I insisted. "Open it. Her clothes are inside."

"But because *you've* removed it," said Tick, "you can't prove it was in Earl's possession."

Liberty put her finger up and stepped forward.

He stopped her in her tracks. "And before you say you can back up what Coop's saying, partners in crime aren't considered reliable witnesses. Earl could say you planted it."

My stomach flip-flopped as his words sunk in. How dumb was I to have taken it from his office? I screwed up. Big-time.

"But Tick," I argued, "how could I have planted it? It's been *missing* for forty years."

Earl shook hands with Gomez, then shuffled toward us in his bathrobe. "Miscreants! Hope you know I'm pressing charges."

I took a step toward him. "You killed my gran!"

Tick pulled me back. "Earl," he held up the suitcase. "How'd you get this?"

Why was Tick asking nicely? Wasn't it obvious Earl stole it?

Earl stopped dead in his tracks.

I could picture it all. Earl would start squirming. Maybe he'd get dry mouth or something. He'd run his hand through his thin, comb-over hair. Then his shoulders would sag as the realization he was caught sunk in. *"You're right. You got me,"* he'd say. *"I did it.*

Tabby discovered I was stealing from the church. She threatened to turn me in. I had to silence her and then I made it look like she ran away..." then he'd drift off into silence. Tick would cuff him and lead him away in his bathrobe and slippers.

"Earl?" Tick gestured to Gomez, who nudged Earl toward us.

Even in the orange light, he looked pale as he stared at the suitcase. "I forgot that was even there," he whispered.

I didn't even know I'd been holding my breath, but, as soon as he said those words, I let out a lungful of air.

From the corner of my eye I could see Tick's shoulders drop, like he was also relieved. At least Earl wasn't going to claim he'd never seen it before or that I'd planted it.

"Earl," Tick crossed his arms and faced him. "You need to tell me—"

"Please don't lock me up! I got the claustrophobia real bad and I—I just panicked," he cried. "I didn't mean for Tabby to die. I tried to warn her, but it was too late! She was already dead when I got there!"

CHAPTER 30

AFTER A MOMENT OF STUNNED silence, Deputy Gomez pulled his handcuffs from his utility belt. "Earl Winston, I'm arresting you for the murder of Tabitha Goodman. You have the right to an attorney—"

"It was an accident! I never meant to kill her. But you gotta understand, I couldn't go to jail. I—I—I *can't* go to jail!" He clung to Tick's arm. "I'll never survive."

Tick raised a brow.

Earl moaned and ran his hands through his hair. "A jail cell. They're so small and—and locked…"

"Earl, what happened? Start from the beginning," Tick said, pulling his black notepad from his front pocket. "Try to remember as much as you can."

Earl sighed. "I haven't forgotten a single thing from that day. But you have to believe me. It was a horrible accident. Tabby came to see me at Comforted Souls late that morning."

Tick clicked his pen. "About what?"

"Gambling. She was furious with Doc."

Wait. What? Gramps didn't gamble.

"Why did she come to you?" asked Tick.

Earl hung his head. "I was his bookie."

That went against *everything* Gramps had ever told me. "That's a lie," I shouted. "Gramps doesn't gamble. It's his rule! He only has two—don't drink and don't gamble! He wouldn't! He won't even buy a raffle ticket."

Mama's brow creased. "Coop's right. Harley's so straitlaced he practically wears a corset. You honestly expect people to believe he's a gambler?"

Earl scoffed. "Maybe not now, but he sure used to. Could put away a few drinks back then as well."

I clenched my fists. "No! Didn't you hear me? That's his other rule! He doesn't! He can't—" My voice cracked.

"Ask him yourself. He didn't always have those rules, now did he?" He shook his head. "If there's something gamblers are good at, it's lying to those around them so they don't find 'em out. There wasn't a horse race or card game anywhere he didn't place a bet on. He might've been the town doctor, but *she* was the one with all the money, and he blew through her cash like a tornado at the U.S. Treasury."

Gomez shot a glance to Tick. "Then what?"

Earl stared at the ground. "Tabby said she and Harley had had a fight. She'd threatened to cut him off. Then she threatened to turn *me* in if I didn't stop acting as his bookie. She was shouting so loud she could've woken Mrs. Simmons laid out in the embalming room. Passersby actually stopped and peered in through the front windows. I begged her to keep her voice down and swore to her I'd stop."

"Sounds like motive to me," said Gomez.

Earl swiveled, his fists opening and closing. "No! We parted on good terms. I gave her some zucchini muffins before she left— as a kind of peace offering."

Gomez raised a brow. "She yells at you about enabling her husband's gambling habit, threatens to turn you in to the police, and you send her home with *muffins*?"

Earl stroked his robe as though it were a fine suit. "I'm an excellent baker. It's always been a hobby. Still is. Ask anyone." But he paled.

"What next?" asked Tick.

"I musta been in too big a hurry." His eyes widened. "Later I saw a box of Balm-A-Body was right next to the baking soda! Maybe I brought it up with me by accident or something." He nearly sobbed the last sentence.

Earl ran his handcuffed hands back and forth through his hair. "I knew I had to warn Tabby right away not to eat the muffins—just in case I'd gotten the powders mixed up. I jumped into the hearse, but when I got to her house… I was too late!"

Justice leaned over to me. "And he wonders why your Mama won't sell his stuff at the store."

Earl let out a moan. "Nuthin' but a coupla plates with crumbs. I panicked. The whole town had heard her screeching threats at me earlier. And worse, the Feather sisters! You know how they gossip. I had a criminal record. There was *no way* people would believe it was an accident."

Earl held up his hands. "I just made it look like she ran off—typed the note on Doc's typewriter. Grabbed some clothes and the suitcase…" He swallowed hard. "The playground had just been put in, I had my hearse, so I did what I had to…" He trailed off. "Afterward I hid her stuff here and tried to forget the whole mess."

"Helped yourself to her necklace too, right, *Lear Stowinn?*" said Beau.

Both Tick and Gomez turned and stared at Beau.

Earl nodded. "I couldn't help myself. Old habits die hard."

"*Told you,*" Beau mouthed smugly to us.

"But the minute her remains were found I knew I had to get rid of it," said Earl. "Having me a record and all I figured the police might come 'round looking to talk to me." He faced me. "Harley and I are about the same height, so I dressed like him and pawned it at the Trash and Treasures in Sangerville. Wasn't easy, let me tell you. He's not a scrawny man. Had to put on a few layers of clothes to pad myself and kept my back to the camera."

"Why not mention Doc's gambling problem in the note?" asked Tick. "After the fight she and Doc had, it would have been an easy sell for Harley."

Earl squirmed. "I wanted to keep quiet about the gambling. Didn't want to risk an investigation. Gambling wasn't legal back then."

"Hate to tell you, but being a bookie isn't legal *now*," muttered Tick.

"That's pretty logical thinking for someone who claims it was an accident," said Gomez.

"It was! You have to believe me." Earl held his arms close to his chest like a scared mouse. He looked at me, his eyes softening. "I'm so sorry, Coop. I didn't mean to kill your grandma. She was one of the few people around town who didn't treat me like dirt." He whimpered something about claustrophobia again, but I couldn't make the words out.

Tick handed the suitcase to Deputy Gomez. "You'll want this to tag into evidence."

Gomez nodded and opened the door of Tick's cruiser. Earl slid in.

"Wait!" I jogged over. "How did your blood end up on her ring?"

Earl looked up from the back seat. "Tabby's kitchen was a wreck. Overturned chairs. Broken glass. Couldn't have it looking that way if I wanted Doc to believe the note. I cut my hand cleaning, and I must've got some on her ring when I moved her body."

Gomez shut the door, then he and Tick walked away and talked for a few minutes. Then Gomez drove off in his own car, leaving Earl handcuffed inside of Tick's.

Tick walked over to where we stood. "You kids are still in trouble for breaking into Earl's—even if it did lead to finding evidence."

I heaved a sigh. "I don't care. Gramps is off the hook, and that's all that matters."

Beau, Justice, and Liberty nodded.

Tick hooked his thumbs into his utility belt and exhaled. "That's where you're wrong, Cooper."

I cocked my head. "What do you mean?"

"Earl just admitted to killing Tabby," said Mama. "I don't understand."

Tick ran his hand over his face. "The poison that killed Tabby was arsenic—which isn't found in Balm-A-Body.

"It is!" I said. "I did research. Embalming stuff used to have arsenic in it. So it totally could've—"

Tick shook his head. "*Used to*, Coop. In the nineteenth century. Don't you think we checked that out? Earl wouldn't have been using anything like that." He nodded toward his car. "He may *think* he killed Tabby, but he didn't. He just buried her."

"So the real murderer is still out there?" I asked.

"Not for long." Tick faced me. "The DA has everything he needs. Being cut off from a fortune is a heavy-duty motive, especially when you're dealing with a compulsive gambler. They'll do anything to keep their addiction going. Pair that with the fact he'd bought the arsenic…"

"What are you saying?" My breath caught in my throat. I couldn't breathe.

Tick's eyes met mine. "Gomez is leaving to arrest your grandfather now."

Mama gasped.

"But he can't!" I said.

He threw his hands up in the air. "He flat-out lied, Cooper. I asked him if there were marital problems, fights, or money issues, and he said *no*. For the love of all that's holy! Gambling checks all three of those boxes!"

CHAPTER 31

I SAT ON THE EDGE of my bed, numb, staring at the case closet wall. Moonlight shined on my notes and photographs, but I didn't care about them anymore. I didn't care about Lear Stowinn or Earl Winston or whatever he wanted to call himself. I didn't care about some bookkeeper forty years ago who might've been stealing money from the church. It had nothing to do with Gran's death. I was done with mysteries. They brought nothing but pain.

Gramps had lied to me. I wanted to punch something, my heart hurt so bad. I hadn't known what betrayal felt like until now. *If there's something gamblers are good at, it's lying to those around them.* Earl's words repeated in my head. He was right. Gramps had lied about the gambling and marriage problems. It's not a stretch to think he lied about being a murderer too. Bile rose in my throat.

Stupid case closet.

Stupid photographs and suspect cards.

Stupid me.

I pushed off the bed. My whole body shook, but I refused to give in to the tears that wanted to fall. I clawed at the papers taped to my closet wall, ripping them all down. Discarded photos and notecards scattered and floated to floor.

Beau rolled over on his mattress. "What are you doing?" he mumbled.

"Nothing." I choked back a sob. "Go back to sleep."

He sat up and leaned against the wall. He remained quiet for several moments, and then broke the silence. "You worried about your gramps?"

I didn't answer. Just stared at the pile of torn papers and pictures at my feet.

I wasn't worried. I was ticked.

"It gets better. You get used to it. That sick feeling in your stomach."

My chest tightened. "He's not who he said he was."

Beau looked out the window. "Most people aren't." After a moment he shoved his covers off and stepped across his mattress. He sat on the window seat. "Hey, man. I get the lying thing. Really."

Beau rested his head against the windowpane. "Lying is when your daddy says he's going to the store for ice cream but comes back with beer. Or when he swears he's not drunk and you pretend to believe him because living with that lie is easier than living with the truth."

I scoffed. "Yeah well, loving your dad when he's the town drunk is different than loving a possible murderer."

Beau's face tightened.

The heat of shame rushed to my face. "Sorry. I shouldn't have said that."

"No, you shouldn't have." He stared back out the window. "But just because your gramps lied doesn't mean he killed his wife. Why are you giving up on him so fast? Think about how long you've known him." He swung his legs down, perched on the edge of the window seat, and faced me. "Do you really believe he's a murderer?"

"Gramps once said trust doesn't come with a refill. When it's gone, you probably won't get it back, and if you do, it's never the same." I looked at Beau. "If that's the case, I'm holding an empty cup." I slumped over to my bed and sat on the edge. "I get why he didn't talk about his past at all. He didn't just have skeletons in his closet. He might've had 'em at the playground too."

I was sick of secrets being kept *and* even sicker when I discovered what they were. I'd always believed Gramps was a man of his word. Brave and trustworthy. But now, was everything a lie? Cowards hid behind lies. Not brave men. Brave men faced the truth and fought the fight. Like my daddy had done. But Daddy was gone. And Gramps, who'd become like my daddy, was gone too.

"If you'd asked me two weeks ago if I could trust Gramps for anything, I'd have said yes." I picked at the threads on my bedspread. "But now…I can't."

Beau stood and walked back to his mattress. "You know, as much as you boast about how your dad was a Marine and never gave up, you sure are giving up on your gramps easily enough. Don't mean you still can't love him. If I only loved people who were perfect, I'd be lonelier than I already am." He pulled the covers up over his shoulder. "Go to sleep, moron." He turned away from me.

Sighing, I took Gran's journal from my side table and read by the moonlight. Her entry must've been after she learned about Gramps's gambling problem. It was dated March 23. The last thing she ever wrote in her journal.

Such a struggle, but I've decided. Tomorrow the truth comes out…Why does the love of money turn good people bad?

She took the words right out of my mouth.

Tick was standing in the kitchen cradling a steaming cup of coffee when I walked in the next morning.

I stopped and glared. "What are *you* doing here?" I shoved my hands into my jeans pockets.

He nodded a greeting. "Morning to you too."

The sudden thought that Tick had changed his mind about not arresting us for last night's episode glued my feet to the wooden floor.

"*Why* are you here?" I said.

Tick didn't answer right away. Instead he took a long draw of coffee and stared over his mug at me. He lowered the cup slowly and sighed. "Your mama asked if I would go with her to see your gramps and his lawyer at the county jail. They're trying to arrange bail and such."

"What about me and Beau? We going too?"

Mama breezed past where I stood in the kitchen doorway. She dropped her purse on the table and set a small suitcase on the floor. "No. Mr. Gordon said he'd look after y'all until I return. You're going to church with him, and he's expecting you at his house in less than an hour. Ride your bikes."

I glanced down at her suitcase. "How long will you be gone?"

She rummaged through her purse. "I'm not sure. A couple days? Maybe longer? It's Sunday. Who knows how slow things will move." She looked up from her purse. "And don't think you're getting off without any punishment after last night's escapade. I've got two words for you. Community. Service."

Images of picking up trash along County Road 95 while wearing a bright orange jumpsuit popped into my head.

Tick smiled into his coffee but remained silent. I figured the community service gig was his idea—it was the kind of irritating thing a deputy would come up with. Mama continued digging through her purse muttering about her car keys.

I swallowed. "What exactly will we be doing?"

"Police clothing drive." She sighed and upturned her purse, dumping everything onto the table.

Definitely Tick's idea.

I guess he took that as his cue to expand on Mama's short answer. "After church, the four of you can go door-to-door and collect whatever folks have put out on their front porch for the drive. Then you can sort through it all and bring it to the police station."

"It's like a hundred degrees out there already," I said. "Do you think maybe we—"

"Would you rather scrape roadkill?" Mama shot back.

Hauling bags of clothing around would be a pain, but it definitely beat roadkill. The humidity was so thick you could wring the air.

Tick put his hand on Mama's shoulder and squeezed it before walking over to the back door. He pulled her keys from where they were stuck in the knob and set them on the table.

She scooped them up and sighed with relief. "I'll meet you in the car."

Tick nodded. "Be right there." He rinsed his mug in the sink, and then he turned around to face me. "One more thing about last night. Before he left, Deputy Gomez asked me to talk to you. He wants you to know if you and your friends interfere with a police investigation again, you will be arrested. And we're not kidding. Stay out of it. For your sake…and your mama's. Do you understand?"

"Yes sir," I said. "Nothing to interfere with now anyway, I guess."

He reached for the doorknob. "I'm sorry, Coop. I really am. I didn't want it to turn out this way, either." And he left.

Beau came down minutes after the door shut, holding the papers and photographs I'd ripped off the closet wall the night before. "What are these?"

I scoffed. "A waste of time."

He dropped them on the table and picked up the top two photos. "Why pictures of ledgers? I mean, obviously someone was stealing money, but why do *you* have them?"

Trust Beau to have figured out within ten seconds of looking at a photo that someone had been stealing. I hated him for being so smart. I snatched the photos out of his hand. "Never mind. It's not important anymore." I folded them up and shoved them in my back pocket. "Come on—we got to get to the Gordons."

CHAPTER 32

PASTOR JOEL SHOOK HANDS WITH Mr. Gordon when we walked inside Windy Bottom Baptist. "When's your wife getting home?"

"Not soon enough," muttered Justice, holding his stomach.

Mr. Gordon rolled his eyes. "Next week."

Pastor Joel grinned. "Hang in there." He peered around Mr. Gordon's shoulder. The smile slid off his face when he saw me. His voice softened. "I'm sorry about your gramps, Coop. We're praying for him and your family."

I stared at the floor as heat drew up my neck. "Thanks."

"And I'm sorry I haven't replied to your email yet. I wasn't the pastor back then, and when the previous one retired, he moved to Florida. Been trying to find the answer for you, but you're better off asking the Feather sisters. You can't spit on the sidewalk without one of them hearing about it. They'd know for sure."

I shrugged. "To tell you the truth, it doesn't much mat—"

"And speak of the devil, here they are." Pastor Joel reached out and took Miss Ruth's hand between his own and pulled her in. "Miss Ruth. Miss Meriwether. Coop has a question for y'all." He turned to me. "Service is about to start, so I need to dash— but let me know what you find." He began to walk away but stopped and turned. "And if there's *anything* your family needs— including your gramps—let us know."

He disappeared through the doorway leading into the sanctuary. Mr. Gordon touched my shoulder. "Don't take too long."

"Yes, sir."

Miss Meriwether peered around the doorway and scowled. "You answer his question, sister. I'm going to grab our pew before some newcomer sits in it."

Miss Ruth turned to me. "Oh, Coop. Such a shock to hear about Harley." She wrapped her arms around me and squeezed. I wasn't going to start crying. At least, that's what I told myself. "An arrest, after all these years." She adjusted the grip on her purse strap. "Now, what did you want to know?"

"It's really not important, Miss Ruth," I said.

"Nonsense. Make me feel needed." She grinned.

My face felt tired from all the fake smiling I'd done since we got to church. Sighing, I jammed my hands into my back pocket and was surprised when they touched paper. I'd forgotten the photos I'd snatched from Beau's hand earlier were there. Why not ask? Might as well. I pulled the photos out, unfolded them, and handed them to Miss Ruth. "I found some photos with Tabby's things. It looks like the church's bookkeeper was, umm," I leaned in to whisper, "stealing from the memorial fund."

She put a hand over her heart as she stared at the photos. "Oh, dear."

"I just wanted to know who the bookkeeper was forty years ago." I shrugged. "It—it actually doesn't matter anymore, but..."

She looked around her and then took a step closer to me. "Who else has seen these?"

Jus and Lib had seen them, and Beau looked briefly that morning but no one who was alive from forty years ago. That's probably what she meant. "No one."

She closed her eyes and sighed. "Well, that's a relief." She clutched my arm and whispered into my ear. "Because the person keeping the books for the church was your grandmother."

Her words punched me in the gut. "What?" My mouth hung open.

"Meriwether was the volunteer bookkeeper, but between

school and tutoring and such, she fell behind. She told me Tabby offered to help her out for a season—they were friends too, you know." She blinked her eyes frantically, and sniffed. "Oh dear, this is horrible." She fumbled with the clasp on her purse, then pulled out a tissue. "So distressing. I didn't know. I mean, I knew there were money troubles." She patted my hand. "Your grandfather's gambling—oh, sugar, don't look so shocked. The whole town was buzzing by daybreak this morning. Things must've gotten bad if she started embezzling the church's funds." She wiped her nose.

I wanted to throw up. My heart dropped to the floor with the weight of her words. Gramps was a liar and Gran was a thief. The family tree was becoming a thornbush.

Miss Ruth grabbed my hands. "Honey bee." She pulled me in close and hugged me tight. "I'm so sorry." Organ music floated through the doors. "The service is starting. Wipe your tears, now, child, and get going. It's nothing a heartfelt prayer can't help… soothe our troubled souls."

I dragged myself down the aisle to where Mr. Gordon sat with Liberty, Justice, and Beau, and slumped into the pew.

Liberty nudged me. "You okay?" she mouthed.

"No."

During the hymns I stood but didn't sing. I didn't hear which book in the Bible to turn to. And I didn't care what Pastor Joel was preaching about. I stared at the floor forever and then at my shoes, lost in my own thoughts. If times were so hard for Gran that she started stealing from the church's memorial fund, why didn't she write about it in her diary? That's what diaries are for, right? Or maybe she did. Maybe that last entry about money turning people bad was about her and *not* Gramps.

My neck grew stiff. When I couldn't stand looking down anymore, I looked up. The answers weren't on the floor anyway.

The stained glass windows glistened in the sunlight. The church had twelve in all. One of the Last Supper, and then one for each disciple—except Judas. You don't get your own window if you're the dude who betrayed the Son of God. He wasn't even in the Last Supper scene—just his plate so at least you knew he'd been there.

The window closest to me had a plaque above it: "*John writing the book of Revelation.*" He sat at a wooden desk, wearing a blue robe, and holding a quill pen in his left hand and a piece of a parchment with writing on it in his right. No smears on the parchment. I mean, *if* John were left-handed there'd be smears across his paper. Duh. Just like with Liberty's schoolwork. Just like in Gran's journal. Every single page she'd written had smudges. Just like in the...no, wait. The...the photo of the ledger...the ledger had *no* smears. It was clean. Not a blur in sight.

I sat up. A spark of hope began to grow in my gut.

Unless Gran had suddenly started writing with her right

hand, no way was she the person stealing from the church. Plus, now that I thought about it, I'd read enough of Gran's journal to know her handwriting. I mean, sure, numbers look different than letters, but there were *some* words in the ledger too—like *Wednesday*. And they didn't match what I'd seen in the journal. The *W*'s in the ledger had a funky little curl at the very top of the letter. Gran didn't write her *W*'s like that—at least I was pretty sure she didn't. I needed to get home and look in her journal.

Miss Ruth was confused. Maybe she'd misunderstood what Miss Meriwether had told her all those years ago. I reached for the photos in my back pocket, but they weren't there. Drat! Miss Ruth still had them.

I faced forward and tried to focus. My ears caught the words "always faithful" from the pulpit. Is that what Pastor Joel was preaching about? Faithfulness?

Semper Fidelis. Always faithful. Daddy had lived out the Marine motto every day. He knew his duty and had never strayed or given up. Had I given up too easily like Beau said? Sure, Gramps *seemed* guilty, but if there was one thing I'd learned lately, it was things weren't what they seemed.

Mama's show of strength was totally bogus. I'm not an idiot. The last few days had really taken their toll on her. She pretended everything was okay. Except she cried behind closed doors and blamed her red eyes on not sleeping well. Gramps wasn't the "keep your nose clean" guy he wanted us to think he was. Gran hadn't abandoned her family. Tick wasn't a traitor. And Beau wasn't a total jerk—at least not all of the time.

Shoot... For all I knew, Earl's muffins actually tasted good.

I *had* to keep fighting. For Dad. And for Gramps.

He might've been a liar, but he wasn't a murderer.

And Gran wasn't the one who did the books.

What really happened forty years ago? I was ready to find out.

~~~

After church, Beau raced ahead to Mr. Gordon's pickup. "I call shotgun," he said climbing up front.

"Mr. Gordon?" I climbed in behind Justice. "I left something at my house. Can we swing by on our way home?"

"I suppose so." He turned on the car. "But don't dawdle. The four of you need to get started on collecting clothes."

"Why were you all squirmy during service?" Liberty slid in next to me. "Did it have anything to do with what Miss Ruth said? 'Cause you slinked in grumpier than a Disney dwarf but then got all twitchy toward the end."

I lowered my voice so Mr. Gordon wouldn't hear. "I was thinking about the murder."

"Did you have an apostrophe?" asked Justice.

"An epiphany, dork brain," said Liberty. "Check your dictionary."

"I just want to grab everything from the case closet. That's all."

Mr. Gordon slowed to a stop outside my house. Liberty opened the door and jumped out. I followed.

"I'll be right back," I called over my shoulder as I jogged to the front door. Once inside, I hurried to the kitchen table and collected all the papers Beau had brought down earlier, and then dashed upstairs to make sure none had been left on my floor. I stuffed everything in a backpack and raced to Mr. Gordon's truck.

CHAPTER 33

LIBERTY AND JUSTICE FOUND THEIR old red wagon in the garage under a pile of Halloween decorations, dirty laundry, and a bag of Chester's dog food. We spent the afternoon loading bags and boxes of clothes into it. Heat floated off the sidewalk in waves, and I had no doubt bacon could've fried on the hood of a car. Sweat trickled down between my shoulder blades. Still, it was better than scraping roadkill. Barely.

After every four or five houses, we'd have to return to the Gordons' to unload. Their living room was filling up fast and it was a good thing Mrs. Gordon was still out of town. Liberty said her mama would've felt having her house buried under a giant pile of mothball-smelling clothes was more of a punishment for her than us.

As we walked, I told them what Miss Ruth had said about Gran stealing from the church. "But it wasn't her. I looked at the handwriting in her journal when we got home from church—it doesn't match, and besides, there were no smears in the ledger."

"Take it from a lefty—there's always smears," said Liberty. "I think your theory makes sense."

"Why would Miss Ruth lie?" Justice let the wagon handle drop as we walked up the steps of Mrs. Garcia's house.

"I don't think she lied on purpose." Two large garbage bags tagged "Clothing Drive" sat next to her door. I grabbed one. "It happened a long time ago. And she said it was Miss Meriwether who told her that Gran was the one keeping the books. Plus, people forget stuff. I mean, like every year, months after Christmas, Mama finds a present she'd hidden for Gramps or me but forgot about."

"Good point," said Liberty. "Our folks forget where they've hidden Christmas presents too."

"My dad forgets Christmas *period*," said Beau.

An awkward silence hung in the air.

Beau and I carried the bags to the wagon and balanced them on top of a box. We were on the final street—the same street the Gordons lived on. We figured it'd be better to work from the outside of town in rather than the other way 'round.

I glanced at the leaning tower in the wagon and counted the

remaining houses. "If everyone's cool carrying stuff from the last couple of houses, I bet this can be our last load."

"So are you going to ask Miss Ruth if she was confused when we get to her house?" asked Liberty.

"Maybe—I don't want to embarrass her," I said. "But I do want to ask for the photos back. When the service started we both split, and I forgot to get them from her."

We added another box and two more small bags to the wagon. Beau and I each held a bag by the time we got to the Feather sisters' house, which was next door to the Gordons'. Thankfully, there was only one smallish box covered in a layer of dust on their porch. Liberty grabbed it and then took my bag. "Get the photos and meet us back home."

"Yeah, and don't take too long, lazy boy," said Beau. "We still got to sort all this."

I knocked on the door as they walked down the rickety steps. Miss Meriwether opened it. She peered around the door to where the box had sat and then to Justice, Liberty, and Beau. "Where's our box walking off to?"

"Next door with everyone else's and then to the police station."

"Good." She stepped onto the porch, letting the door close behind her. "Now pay attention, Cooper."

"It's just Coop, ma'am."

She ignored me and continued. "I put a detailed list of what was in our donation box. I want Deputy Vidler to sign off on it. The IRS doesn't care a horse's heinie if those things have been sitting in a box in our attic for eons, and I need that tax write-off. Understand?"

"Yes, ma'am."

She stared at me. "Well, why are you still standing here?"

Miss Ruth opened the door and peeked out. "I knew I heard voices out here. Hello, Coop, dear."

I swallowed. "Umm...I just had a question for Miss Ruth. But I can come back later—"

Miss Ruth waved at hand at her sister. "Oh, don't mind Miss Sourpuss right now. She just needs her afternoon nap."

I was clueless why adults liked afternoon naps. Must be something that comes with age.

Miss Meriwether harrumphed and walked back inside.

"I was wondering, Miss Ruth, if I could have the photos back I showed you this morning? It's just, you know, they belonged to Gran and I have so little of anything that's hers..."

Her hands flew to her mouth. "Oh, Coop! I...I don't know what to say except that I—I don't have them anymore."

"Sure you do. I accidently left them with you at church this morning."

She shook her head, her brows pinched together in worry. "They're gone now."

"What do you mean?"

"Oh no, no, no," she moaned. "I am *so* sorry." She took a deep breath and placed both hand on my shoulders. "I burned them."

"You…you wh—you *burned* them?" I stared in stunned silence.

She stepped out onto the porch and closed the door behind her. "I—I figured after learning what they meant—about your grandmother—that *you'd* want to get rid of them. And, and so did I! Tabby was my best friend, and she didn't needed to be remembered for stealing. That evidence had to be destroyed. I had *no idea* you'd want them back." She grasped both my hands. Her eyes searched my own. "I am so sorry. But you understand, right? Will you ever forgive me?"

Disbelief chewed away at my insides. How could she have destroyed them?

"Coop?" Miss Ruth's voice sounded thin but full of worry all at the same time. "I'm sorry." She opened the door to go back into the house.

I nodded and turned to walk away but stopped and swiveled back. "Miss Ruth?"

"Yes, dear?" She looked over her shoulder.

"Are you sure that was Gran's handwriting?"

"Yes, dear. I asked Meriwether. She wouldn't lie about something like that." She shut the door.

CHAPTER 34

MOST OF THE CLOTHES HAD been dumped out on the living room floor. A few unopened boxes or bags remained. Things were being tossed into larger boxes marked "pants," "sweaters," "dresses," "shirts," "shoes," and "random stuf"—spelled with one *f*, which meant Justice had done the labeling. A sweater, pitched by Liberty, landed at my feet. "Not quite the same as a baseball, but it'll do," she said with a grin.

I picked it up. "You're not gonna believe this. Miss Ruth burned the photos."

Liberty's jaw dropped. "Why would she do that?"

"Yeah," huffed Beau. "That doesn't look suspicious at all."

Justice gathered a bunch of pants in his arms and dropped them in the pants box. "I still have the negatives. We'll print new ones."

I breathed in a sigh of relief and told them what Miss Ruth said about the photographs.

Beau wrinkled his face. "I'm not buying it." He chucked a pair of shoes into a nearby box. "Maybe Miss Meriwether wanted her sister to *think* it was Tabby. What if ol' Meriwether was the crook, and she was just covering her tracks? It's not like Tabby can defend herself or anything. And, after all, Miss Meriwether has always droned on and on about how little money she has. If anyone were going to filch from the memorial fund, it'd be her and not your ridiculously rich grandmother."

"She wasn't rich after Doc gambled away all her money," Justice pointed out.

"Dude." Liberty stopped and stared at him. "Whose side are you on?"

"What's that saying?" asked Justice, grabbing a shirt. "Money is the root of all evil?"

"No." Beau faced him. "It's the *love* of money is the root of all evil. It's from the Bible."

We all turned and stared at him.

"What?" he said. "I read."

But his words poked a memory. "Hold on. What did you just say?"

"I said, *I read.*"

"No, before that."

"The love of money is the root of all evil?"

"Yes, that! Wait here." I dashed off to Justice's room and found Gran's diary in with my overnight bag and hurried back. I flipped to the entry I'd read the night before—the last one she ever wrote. "Listen to this. '*Such a struggle, but I've decided. Tomorrow the truth comes out. Why does the love of money turn good people bad?*'" I closed her journal. "At first I thought she was talking about Gramps's gambling habit. But," my pulse quickened, "what if this was about finding the fake ledger instead? The dates on the ledger and the diary entry are the *same*."

"Hmm." Beau chewed the side of his mouth. "If she decided she was going to tell the police what she'd found and told the thief her plan, that's a strong motive for sure."

"Hold on." Liberty scooped up an armful of shirts and peeked over the pile at me. "Maybe we should figure out what we *know* for sure before we get carried away. Grab paper and a pen, Coop. We'll sort clothes and tell you what to write."

"Why can't I write and Coop sort?" asked Justice.

"Because you can't spell worth a lick," said Beau. "Do you think we're stupid?"

Liberty turned to Justice. "Don't answer that—it's rhetorical."

He reached for his dictionary.

Moments later, I was sitting on the sofa. I grabbed a book to put under my paper. "Okay, talk to me."

Liberty held up a pair of jeans large enough to fit all four of us. "We know someone was stealing from the church, and Tabby also knew about it."

"And we know she was going to talk to that person the same day she died," said Beau.

"How do you know that?" asked Justice.

Beau pointed to the journal next to me. "Because she said 'the truth comes out tomorrow,' and that was her last entry. She died the next day."

Justice was silent for a moment, then shook his head. "Yeah, but that doesn't mean she's going to talk to the person. Maybe she meant she was going to go to the police."

"Good point, Jus," said Liberty.

"All right, so she may not have talked to the police, but she was going to tell *someone* the truth."

I wrote fast.

"Umm… She was killed with arsenic." Liberty shuddered.

"And she ate Earl's muffins," added Justice.

I stopped scribbling and looked at him. "Yeah. But they didn't kill her."

"I know. But it's still a mystery why anyone would eat them."

Liberty threw a bathrobe at him. He grinned and slipped it on.

"Another thing is by the time Earl arrived, the place was a wreck, and she was already dead," I said.

Beau held up a duffel bag. "What do I do with this?"

"Open it?" suggested Justice.

Beau dropped it on the floor and unzipped it, but instantly whipped his head back with a grimace. "I think we got someone's nasty gym clothes by mistake."

I snickered. "Might want to set that outside."

He held the bag at arm's length and walked to the front door. "If arsenic smelled this bad, your gran would've noticed it for sure. I read it's a pretty nasty way to kick the bucket. Especially if you're given a megadose. Lots of flailing around, loss of muscle control, and spasms. I bet that's why the place was such a mess."

My hand was cramping I was scribbling so fast. At least I could read my handwriting…sort of. "What else? Anything?"

"Well," Liberty rested a hand on her hip. "Practically everyone in town had access to some form of arsenic."

"And we know who *didn't* do it," said Justice. "It wasn't Earl or Burma—"

Beau shut the front door and turned to me. "And we know it isn't your grandma's handwriting in the ledger."

I added the last comment, then set the paper and pen down. "We have a lot of stuff on this list. Now we gotta figure out how it was done. Forget our old theories about revenge or wanting Gramps to remarry. I think the real motive was silencing Gran before she could turn the thief in. We find the thief, we find the killer."

"Dude, time to get off your butt." Justice flung something across the room. A streak of orange flew through the air and landed on my head. "Make yourself useful. You can talk and sort at the same time."

I pulled off whatever it was and started to throw it back at Justice but stopped. "Where did you find this?" I held up the dress.

"Why? You like it? I don't think it's your size," said Beau.

Liberty snorted.

"We're standing knee-deep in donated clothes from the whole town, and you wanna know where one dress came from? Give me a break," said Justice.

"It's important." I grasped it and hurried over, making my way through the mounds of clothes scattered all over the floor to where he stood. "This dress belonged to Gran. I recognize it from a picture I have of her. Which box did you find it in?"

Justice looked at the boxes and bags opened all around his feet. "I don't know. It was from one of these. I remember seeing shoes in the same box. What's the big deal anyway?"

I held up a pair. "Were these the shoes?"

"Or these?" asked Liberty.

"Sorry." Justice shrugged. "They all look the same to me."

Beau bent down and pulled a pair of black shoes and a slip of paper from a box. "Looks like the dress came from the stuff Miss Meriwether gave you." He read from the paper. "One green dress. One winter coat, wool. Four pairs of shoes, size eight. One orange-and-white dress."

"Her tax receipt!" I took it from his outstretched hand.

"Why is the dress important?" Justice's face scrunched in confusion.

I ran my hands through my hair. "I don't know, but I feel like it is. That was Gran's favorite dress, which was missing from the rest of her belongings after she died, and it was in with Miss Meriwether's things. Doesn't that seem suspicious?"

Beau shrugged. "How do you know it's your grandma's dress? Maybe Meriwether had the same one."

I shook my head. "Not this kind—it was awfully expensive." I flipped the dress to the front and looked at the buttons. A *G* and *R* intertwined with each other. I tried to remember what Mama had said about the designer. What was his name? It was foreign-sounding. Gustavo? Gianni? Giovanni… That was it! Giovanni Rue.

"Maybe Tabby gave it to her?" suggested Liberty. "People do that, right?"

"But Gramps said this was her *favorite*. She wore it on their honeymoon. I don't think she'd just give away a dress that cost over a thousand dollars. Do you?" I sighed. "I don't know how it fits in with the murder, but something tells me it's important."

"Is it just me, or does everything seem to lead back to Miss Meriwether?" asked Beau.

Mr. Gordon, who'd been outside cutting the grass, walked into the living room with raised brows.

"It's more organized than it looks," said Liberty.

He frowned and sniffed the air, then under each arm. "What do I smell?"

"Decades-old mothballs and sweat," said Beau. His eyes widened. "I—I don't mean you, though…sir. I found a gym bag earlier."

Mr. Gordon chuckled. "Y'all almost done? I thought I'd do something special for dinner—"

Justice whimpered.

"—and get pizza."

Justice exhaled.

"We're almost done," Liberty said. "Can you drive us to the police station so we can drop it all off?"

Mr. Gordon nodded. "Load the truck while I'm in the shower. We'll grab the pizza on our way back home." He turned and left.

"Leave the dress," I said. "As far as I'm concerned, it's evidence."

"What about Miss Meriwether's list?" asked Beau.

"We have to turn that in for Tick to sign." I took out my phone from my pocket. "But I'm photographing it first. That way they can't deny they ever had the dress."

CHAPTER 35

I TURNED LIKE A ROTISSERIE chicken all night thinking about Miss Meriwether. My brain wouldn't turn off. When I finally did fall asleep, my dreams were filled with dresses, fake ledgers, and one enormous llama. Everything made sense except the llama. But I had a theory—about the case.

I filled Justice, Liberty, and Beau in as we walked to school Monday morning. "It goes back to the idea that things aren't what they seem to be. From the beginning we'd assumed whoever killed Gran *also* staged stuff to make it look like she ran off. But now we know that's not what happened. It was two *different* people. One who killed her, and another who buried her—Earl."

Liberty tossed her baseball in the air and caught it. "So maybe the murderer *wanted* the body to be found?"

I nodded. "I think Gran called Miss Meriwether, told her

she knows she's stealing and she's going to turn her in. All Miss Meriwether had to do was poison her with the rat poison she already had, then wait for Gramps to come home from the clinic and discover her body. She was probably hoping Gramps would be arrested for the murder. Then, not only would she not have to worry about the theft from the memorial fund being discovered, but she'd also get revenge for Gramps dumping her sister."

Justice nodded. "Smacking two mosquitoes with one slap."

"What about the dress?" asked Beau.

"I'm still working on that, but I have a hunch it ties in somewhere."

"There's only one problem," said Liberty, catching her ball.

"What?" I asked.

We jogged across the street to the schoolyard.

"Tabby was killed during the day, and Miss Meriwether would've been at school surrounded by students. There's no way she could've snuck out and killed Tabby."

"That's where you come in," I said.

Liberty looked sideways at me. "How?"

"When you're in the library this morning, I need you to look up something."

"What?"

"We know Gran died March 24, 1977. Find out when spring break was that year," I said.

"You thinking school was out the same week Tabby died?" Beau asked.

"I'm hoping."

Liberty shrugged. "That should be easy. The library has a copy of every yearbook starting from like, *forever* ago, and they always include the school calendar. I know that 'cause I'm always reshelving them. People like to look through them and make fun of the teachers' pictures." She snorted. "You should see Coach Iseminger's photo—his toupee was sliding off just as they took his picture."

"Then what will you do?" asked Justice.

"Not sure," I said. "I should probably tell Tick about the ledger photos. He's going to be super mad I didn't tell him earlier, though. Mama will flip too. Let's just say goodbye now, because I'll be grounded until I'm twenty-one."

Liberty whistled.

Justice looked over his shoulders as if he was making sure no one was nearby. "What about the ledger photos? Want me to print off another set?"

"Yes," I said.

"And put them in a safe place," said Beau. "Those could help your gramps. A good lawyer can make an argument that the handwriting introduces 'reasonable doubt' that he's the killer. Someone else had a strong motive for wanting your gran dead besides him."

"*He* didn't *want* her dead," I grumbled, climbing the school steps.

Beau looked at me. "You know what I mean."

~~~~

"Hey, Tick." I swallowed and gripped the phone. The afternoon sun poured into Justice's room, but the heat engulfing me had more to do with nerves. "Before I say too much, in my defense, I didn't know I was interfering at the time, so please don't arrest me." The words seemed to trip and fall over each other as I spewed the out.

"What are you talking about?" said Tick.

Taking a deep breath, I told him all about finding Gran's camera with the film and how Justice developed it—twice. And about discovering her diary mixed in with Dad's books. I kept talking so he wouldn't have a chance to yell.

"What was on the film?" asked Tick.

"Mostly boring stuff from the church—stained glass windows and flower arrangements, that sort of thing, except for a couple." I explained the images of the last two photos on the roll. "It looked like someone was stealing from the church."

He listened without interrupting as I shared Gran's last diary entry and how it had the same date as the church ledger. "I don't think her death had *anything* to do with Gramps's gambling."

I told him how Miss Meriwether told her sister it was Gran

who'd done the bookkeeping. "But that's a total lie, because Gran was left-handed. One look at her diary will prove that—'cause of the smears. And there's no smears in the ledger." I gripped the phone tighter. "Plus, it doesn't even look like her writing."

There was silence on the other end. I didn't know if he was angry with me for keeping all of this information, or if he was just thinking.

"Tick? I'm sorry I didn't tell you about the photos or the diary. But we have a theory. I think when Gran was photographing things at the church, she came across the ledgers. Justice developed another set of the pictures at school today. Check your phone—I'm sending them to you now." I hit the button and sent them, then continued where I left off. "Maybe she recognized the handwriting—but I reckon Miss Meriwether killed Gran to keep her from going to the police. If we could just look at her bank account or—"

"Coop," Tick interrupted. "Coop, listen. I'm driving and I can't look at any pictures right now."

"But Tick—"

"Hold on. That doesn't mean I won't look. I promise as soon as I get back to Windy Bottom, I'll examine them. I want to help Harley. I really do. But I gotta go—like I said, I'm driving, and I need to focus. I'll look at the photos as soon as I can."

The line went dead. Glaring, I threw my phone on Justice's bed.

CHAPTER 36

"SORRY, DUDE," SAID JUSTICE, STARING at my phone. "Guess he didn't like your theory?"

I flopped on to the bed. "He just can't look at the pictures right now."

"What else can you do?" Liberty leaned over to spit in Justice's trash can, then rested her head against the doorway. "By the way, you were right. There was no school the week Tabby was murdered."

I pounded the mattress. "Gramps is in jail for a murder he didn't commit. Miss Ruth is living with a killer and has been asking questions about the ledger. What if Miss Meriwether thinks her sister might figure things out? She's killed once—she could do it again. Miss Ruth might be in danger."

"You think we should warn her?" asked Beau, looking out the window. "Because it looks like Ol' Grouchy is away from her house."

I hustled off the bed and rushed to the window, along with Liberty and Justice. Miss Meriwether gripped her purse and marched down the sidewalk toward the center of town.

"It's now or never." I dashed to Justice's desk. Earlier I'd added the ledger reprints to the other stuff from the case closet. I sifted through the stack, grabbing the photos, the poison registry list, and Gran's diary. I stuffed them in my backpack. What else? I didn't know.

"What are you doing?" asked Justice.

"I might need these to convince Miss Ruth her sister is a thief and murderer."

"I'm coming with you," said Beau.

Liberty and Justice exchanged glances.

"We can't," said Liberty, her shoulders dropping. "That's what I came up to tell you. Dad just called and told Jus and me to come up to the bookstore."

"But," said Justice, "if that's where Miss Meriwether is headed, we'll distract her and keep her there as long as we can. You'd better hurry!"

I rang the doorbell then stepped back.

"Nervous?" asked Beau.

My insides jittered like they were on a wooden roller coaster.

The kind that rattled so much you wondered if you might've swallowed some teeth during the ride. But I don't think I was nervous. It felt more like I was…ready.

Miss Ruth swung the door open wide. "Coop and Beau—two of my most favorite visitors." She stepped aside. "Come on in. Head to the kitchen and I'll pour you some sweet tea. And I made a new mustard today—you must try it."

Beau followed me down the hallway. We both sat, and I rested my backpack next to me on the floor. A small bouquet of flowers poked out from one of Miss Ruth's old mustard jars in the center of the table. Miss Ruth bustled in behind us and poured three glasses of tea.

"Now," she said, joining us, "to what do I owe the pleasure of your company?" She set the drinks on the table.

I swallowed. How was I supposed to warn her? "Miss Ruth, I think you're in danger," I blurted.

"Danger?" She stopped bringing her tea to her mouth midway. "From what, dear?"

"Your sister."

She gave a bark of laughter and set her glass down. "I'll grant you, Meriwether can be mean enough that a snake couldn't bite her without dying, but I assure you she's no threat to me."

"No, really, Miss Ruth," I pleaded. "She's not who you think she is."

She reached out and patted my hand. "She's an overbearing sibling. That's who she is."

I sighed and looked at Beau. He glanced down to the backpack, then to me. I nodded and pulled it up to my lap. "There's something I want to show you, Miss Ruth."

I unzipped my bag. The diary was on top. I pulled it out and opened to Gran's last diary entry. "This is Gran's diary. The date on her last entry matches the same date as the last entry in the false ledger—in those photos I showed you. Listen to what she wrote." I read it to her and looked up. "I know Meriwether told you it was Gran's handwriting, but it wasn't." I faced the diary toward her. "Look. The writing doesn't match. Plus, Gran was left-handed."

"She was?" Miss Ruth asked. "I had no idea." She shook her head. "Strange, the things we don't know about our friends until they're gone. But sadly, we don't have the photos anymore to verify the handwriting, love."

"That's okay, Miss Ruth." I reached into my bag. "We had the negatives. Justice made another set." I moved the mustard jar of flowers out of my way toward Beau and slid the photos across the table to her.

"The negatives?" She picked up the pictures. Her hand shook as she examined them. And... Did she turn pale?

"It must have been your sister who was stealing, and she just told you it was Gran to cover her tracks," I said.

Miss Ruth kept staring at the photos. I didn't know if she was listening to me or not.

"Miss Ruth?"

She slumped in her chair but didn't look up at me.

"I think your sister killed Gran before she could go to the police." I tapped the diary. "It makes total sense when you put the diary and ledger entries together. And Miss Meriwether bought rat poison too." I brought out the printed poison registry we'd found online and showed Miss Ruth. "I don't know what Miss Meriwether's handwriting looks like, but figured you do. You *do* recognize it, don't you?"

"Yes, child," she whispered. "I recognize it. And you have no idea how much my heart is breaking." She closed her eyes and breathed in deep.

Guilt tugged at me for making her feel so terrible, but *she* was the grandma I never had, and I wasn't going to let another loved one get hurt. Beau sat quietly next to me, fidgeting with the flowers in the mustard jar.

Miss Ruth lightly slapped both hands on the table. "I'm going to make myself a sandwich, and I'm going to make you two detectives something too." She sniffed. "After all, misery loves company, and I'm feeling pretty miserable right now."

She gave us a weak smile, pushed her chair back, and walked to the counter.

Beau rubbed his hands together and looked at me. "I like her sandwiches," he whispered.

The sunlight poured through her kitchen windows, making the marble-filled mustard jars sparkle like stained glass windows. Their colors splashed across the open pages of Gran's diary. I thought of the windows at church. The disciples and the scene from the Last Supper.

Beau slid the mustard jar vase back and forth between his hands.

"Gimme that," I said, taking it away. "You're gonna break it."

"Did you say something, dear?" Miss Ruth called over her shoulder.

"Nothing, Miss Ruth," I said, setting the vase back in the center. My eyes caught the name of the mustard on the label. Miss Ruth loved talking about mustard. Maybe I could lift her mood a little before we all headed to the police to turn in her sister. I read the scrawled label. "Wasabi Wowzer, huh? Is this a new recipe you're trying, Miss Ruth?"

Her back was to me, but she nodded. "Yes—I think I'll enter that one in this year's Pioneer Days festival. I'm still tweaking the recipe." She paused but didn't turn around. "I'm making a special version of it for you boys right now."

The w's looked...funny. I squinted and brought the jar closer. W's...with what looked like an extra swirl.

An extra swirl...Where had I seen w's like that?

I reached across the table for the ledger photo. *Wednesday, March 23.*

No. It was a fluke. A coincidence. Miss Meriwether must've written the label for her. Maybe if I had something else to check it against.

But wait. I did.

The map Miss Ruth gave Beau! The inscription on the back. The photo from the attic was still on my phone. I pulled it from my pocket.

"What are you doing?" asked Beau.

"Hold on." I scrolled through the photos. *To Cordelia— Welcome to Windy Bottom High. Have a great year. Ruth Feather.* Two *w*'s, each with an extra swirl at the top.

That couldn't be. Miss Ruth was like my grandma. She was…nice. Thoughtful. Kind. After all, she gave Beau the map so he would have something of his mama's. But…it must be. Right? My breath caught in my throat. Blood pounded through my ears. *Miss Ruth* was the thief? *She's* the one who'd tried to blame it on Gran? But if it really was Miss Ruth's handwriting in the church ledger, that meant she also—

It was all coming together.

Gran didn't want to turn her best friend in for stealing. *Such a struggle, but I've decided. Tomorrow the truth comes out…Why does the love of money turn good people bad?*

Thoughts tumbled through my head. Gran wrote in her

journal how she and Miss Ruth often ate ham-and-mustard sandwiches together. Miss Ruth said the same thing.

Tabby was such a good sport about trying new flavors.

Ham-and-mustard sandwiches?

I looked up at Miss Ruth.

Mustard. She was mixing mustard.

Everything I *thought* pointed to Miss Meriwether, actually pointed to…Miss Ruth.

There were two plates on the counter for Beau and me. But where was her plate?

I ran my thumb over the label. A sick stew of dread, anger, and fear mixed in my stomach. I slowly raised my eyes. They met Miss Ruth's. She stood next to the table. I never even heard her walk over. She held two plates.

Earl's words rang through my head. *When I got to her house I was too late! Nuthin' but a coupla plates with crumbs.*

A couple of plates.

"Eat up, boys." She set them in front of us. "It will lift my spirits. Don't disappoint me, now."

"Thanks Miss Ruth." Beau picked his up with both hands. "I'm starving. Mr. Gordon isn't a great cook. Anything tastes better than what he makes."

"Crumbs…a couple of plates." I stared at the white bread. Then up at Miss Ruth.

She wasn't kind and grandmotherly. She was cold and calculating. A thieving murderer.

"Go on, Coop," she crooned. "I made those special...just for you."

Beau raised the sandwich to his mouth.

"Coop?" Miss Ruth's smile formed a thin line. "Don't forget your manners. Eat."

I slapped the sandwich out of Beau's hand.

"What the—?"

"Don't eat it!" I stood, knocking over my chair. "Run!"

CHAPTER 37

I SPRINTED DOWN THE HALL.

Beau stumbled after me. "What the heck's going on?"

Everything in my head screamed to run from the House of Lies and never return.

"Where do you think you're going?" Miss Ruth hollered after us. "Get back here!"

I crashed into the front door and yanked on the knob, but the door didn't budge. My fingers felt fat and clumsy as they fumbled to turn the tiny lock. "We got to get out of here!"

"Move over." Beau pushed me aside and twisted the lever, then jerked open the front door.

Tick stood there, hat in one hand and the other raised as though he were about to knock.

"Tick!" I cried.

"Hello, Coop." If he was surprised to see us there, it didn't show on his face. "What are you doing here?"

Miss Ruth hurried after us. "They came over for sandwiches. It's not a good time, Vidler. Come back later." She shoved the door shut.

But Tick put his arm out. "This can't wait, Miss Ruth." He held up a folder. "I came to ask you about discrepancies within the church's memorial fund," he said without a hitch.

Color drained from Miss Ruth's face.

My jaw dropped. I turned to Tick. "You looked at the photos?"

Tick nodded. "The minute I got to the station. Like I promised. A lot of what you said made sense—when I finally *knew* about the diary and the photographs. I cross-referenced the church accounts with the uh, 'personal' deposits—all made to Ruth Feather's account."

I jumped. "I knew it!"

"Just for the record," said Beau. "I knew it too."

Tick looked at Miss Ruth. "And besides needing to talk to you about the church embezzlement," he paused and looked at me, "I also have a few questions about the murder of Tabitha Goodman."

Miss Ruth splayed her hand across her chest. "Have you run

mad? I had nothing to do with her murder! It was Earl. He even admitted to it."

"No." Tick shook his head. "He just *thought* he killed her. She died from acute arsenic poisoning, not from anything he'd done."

"Then it was Harley!" Miss Ruth cried. "How dare you accuse me in my own house!"

"We could go down to the police station," offered Tick.

She breathed in sharply. "I have *never* bought arsenic in my life."

"But your sister did," I said.

"So now you're accusing *me* of murder?" Miss Ruth's hands gripped each other in a fist. Mama always clenched her hands like that when she was hotter than a wood burner.

"Where were you the day Tabby died?" Tick asked, ignoring the glare from Miss Ruth.

"Don't be absurd." She huffed. "I was a teacher—I would've been in school, *surrounded* by my students all afternoon. Not off poisoning someone."

"Actually," Beau stepped forward. "Liberty discovered spring break was the same week Tabby died. There was no school."

Miss Ruth gasped.

Tick pulled out his handcuffs. "Ruth Feather, you're under arrest on suspicion of murder and embezzlement."

CHAPTER 38

HOURS LATER, AFTER DINNER, TICK sat in the Gordons' living room. A plate with a slice of burned apple pie balanced in his lap, and thanks to the open windows, the smoky haze from the kitchen had almost disappeared.

"Wait. Go back to what you just said." I settled down in the sofa next to him. On the coffee table in front of us was everything from my case closet. Ripped-up photos and everything. "I want to make sure I heard you right."

"I *said* Ruth finally admitted to killing your grandmother. She was a tough nut to crack, though."

"Miss Ruth. Funny, sweet Miss Ruth," said Justice. "It's hard to believe she's a killer."

Mr. Gordon shook his head. "Just goes to show you. Did she say why she did it?"

Tick nodded. "Said Tabby discovered she'd was embezzling from the church and was going to turn her in. Ruth told her she'd come over and talk about it. She knew Meriwether had the rat poison, so she poured some into the mustard and made sandwiches."

I clenched my fists. "And then took them to Gran's."

"Yes, but didn't eat any herself." Tick squeezed my shoulders. "She went in through the back door so no one would see her enter and poisoned Tabby with the sandwiches to keep her from going to the police."

"What about the dress we found?" asked Liberty.

Tick took a deep breath. "According to Ruth, after Tabby was dead, she tried to leave the same way she came—through the back door—but workman were in the alley. So she put on one of Tabby's dresses, sunglasses, and a hat. She stuffed her own dress in her handbag and left by the front door. Figured if anyone saw her they'd just think it was Tabby. She changed back into her own dress at the gas station."

"Makes sense." I looked at Liberty and Justice. "Remember how we said they looked alike?"

They nodded.

Beau picked up the photo of Gran from the coffee table. "From a distance, she could definitely pass for your grandmother. But why did Miss Ruth keep the dress?"

Tick set his untouched pie on the table and leaned back

into the sofa. "I asked her that too. She stuffed it in a box of old clothes and asked Meriwether to take the box to the thrift store. Ruth didn't know the box ended up in the attic. She thought that dress was *long* gone." He chuckled. "I suppose once y'all started collecting for the clothing drive, Meriwether went up to the attic and found the box and handed it over. She had no idea it held incriminating evidence against her sister."

The next morning Gramps and I sat on the top step of the front porch, each holding a cup of coffee and staring out at the field across from the house.

"I'm sorry, Coop." He put his arm around my shoulders and squeezed. "I'm sorry I didn't trust you."

His voice sounded like weak coffee. Thin and tired. "I was afraid if I ever told you about the gambling and drinking and broken promises that—" he choked.

I leaned into him. "That I wouldn't love you as much?"

I felt his nod. Reaching up, I squeezed his hand and didn't let go. I loved the weight of his arm resting across the back of my neck and shoulders. The last several days I'd missed his warmth.

"When your daddy died I felt so…alone. Tabby had left years ago—I thought. I had no one." He ran his free hand over his face. Maybe he hoped to wipe the sadness of the memory away. "But then you and your sweet Mama came here to be with me. Here," he repeated. "You could've gone anywhere in the world, but you chose *me*." Gramps cleared his throat. "And I never wanted anything to happen that would risk losing the joy you brought back to me."

Gramps had insecurities? He'd always seemed so strong and brave. How could a man who'd raised Daddy to be a Marine, a hero, be anxious about anything?

He continued. "So instead of trusting you with the truth and trusting you'd love me in spite of my imperfections, I said nothing and kept those hard-earned lessons a secret tucked away deep in my heart," he said. "And for that *I'm* sorry."

"I guess none of us really belong on a pedestal, huh?" I leaned into him. "The truth of the matter is, I *was* mad at first. But..." I let out a slow breath, "I suppose it's kinda like what you're always telling me. Life is a journey, and who we are *now* isn't necessarily who we *will* be, right?"

"You can say that again."

I thought for a moment. "So I guess part of that journey also means who we once *were* isn't necessarily who we are *now*."

He stared into his coffee and let a small laugh escape his lips. "How'd you get to be so smart? But you know what? I wouldn't change any of this mess for the world. Not from Tabby's remains being uncovered to me being arrested. That sounds pretty crazy, doesn't it?"

"Uh, yeah. How come?"

"Because those events showed you who I really was back then. And our past is part of that journey of life. I shouldn't have tried to hide that. And, through it all, you still loved me. It takes a great amount of strength to love people for who they are, but even more to love them for who they aren't. You've got strength in you, Coop."

He gave my shoulder a final hug and cradled his mug with both hands. "So...what do you want know about your Gran or me? I'm an open book."

"What was she like?"

He smiled. "She was remarkable. When we first met, I had no idea she came from money. She never held her wealth above other people. It wasn't even until after I proposed that she told me about her inheritance. I never took her for an heiress."

"Wow." I guess that was another case of something not being what it first appeared to be. "What did you do?"

"Panicked a bit. I told her I didn't want her thinking I was marrying her for her money. She told me I was being silly."

"How'd y'all meet?"

He smiled at the memory. "We sat next to each other the first day of some art history course."

I rubbed my hands together. "Is that when you started gambling? When you were in college?"

He let out a small laugh. "I didn't have two nickels to rub together in college. It wasn't until we married and moved back here that I started gambling."

"Why? You obviously didn't need the money."

Gramps nodded. "You're right. It started off just as a way to relax, blow off steam. Your daddy had just been born, and things were chaotic at home. One night, Earl invited me to a poker game with some other guys. It was fun. Then, instead of one night a week, it was two or three. Then I started betting on football games, horse races. Any sport on TV really. But all it did was create problems. Not financial ones, although I'm not stupid enough to think that wouldn't have eventually happened." He let out a long breath of air. "The gambling caused problems in our marriage. In our relationship."

"Did Gran know?"

"At first, no one except Earl knew. He handled my bets."

"How'd she find out?" I asked.

Gramps stared out at the field. "I accidently left some gambling slips in my pocket. She was so upset when she found them. We yelled. Said terrible things to each other."

I'd seen the vein pop out in Gramps's neck when he got mad, but I'd never heard him yell before. He must've been a totally different person all those years ago.

"She threatened to take Steven unless I got my act together." He sat quietly for a moment. "When she said those words, it felt like I was being swallowed by darkness. She and your dad were my world. I don't know what I would've done if they weren't part of it." He picked up his mug and took a drink. "I promised her that day I'd *never again* gamble. Our family was too precious to me."

The realization of his words hit me. "I'll be right back. Wait here."

I ran inside and up to my room. In my bookcase, tucked inside the middle pages of Gran's journal, was the small repaired wedding photo of Gran and Gramps. The one with *Never Again* scrawled across the back. I jogged back down the stairs and outside.

"This is yours." I laid the photo in his hand then leaned against the column of the porch.

"Good Lord." Gramps looked up at me in surprise. "Where did you find this?"

"It was all in pieces—caught behind your sock drawer. I taped them back together. It was that day I got suspended for fighting. I was worried maybe it had something to do with Gran's murder."

Gramps flipped the photo over and brushed his fingers across the message. He let out a big huff of air. "The day Tabby 'ran away' I sat in my office at the clinic and pulled this photo from my wallet. I wrote those words on the back, then slid it in right next to my money as a reminder of the promise I'd made to Tabby." He shook his head. "But she never knew I did that. I came home that evening and found she'd left… I got mad." He let out a big puff of air. "I ripped the photo to shreds. I have no idea how all the pieces ended up shoved behind the dresser drawer."

A trail of ants wrapped around the bottom of the column and moved toward my coffee mug.

"What about her money? What did you do with it all?"

"I kept expecting her to withdraw it. But she never touched it…obviously. Then I figured she meant for me to use it to take care of your daddy, so I hired a housekeeper. She watched him for me while I was at the practice until he was older. Then I put the remainder in a trust for him. He got everything after he married." Gramps tussled my hair. "It went to your mama when he died. That was how she first opened the coffee shop."

It had never occurred to me how Mama was able to afford the renovations to turn her coffee shop into A Latté Books.

I picked up my mug. "How come you never remarried?"

Gramps sat still, his hands interlaced and resting across his lap. "I kept hoping Tabby would come back. I never gave up that dream."

The ants circled around where my coffee cup used to be, probably wondering where it went. I dipped my finger into my cup and let a few drops fall on the sidewalk. No one should be completely without coffee in the morning. Not even ants.

My thoughts drifted to Miss Ruth. I'd always thought she was a kind, sweet lady. She'd remembered my birthday and Christmas each year. Baked me cookies. Just like a grandma.

One more reminder that the strongest of hearts may be dragged down by the biggest burdens, the meanest of people often hide the deepest hurts, and the kindest of eyes can disguise the cruelest secrets.

"Gramps?"

"Hmm?"

"What will happen to Miss Ruth?"

He let out a long sigh. "Oh, Coop. She's guilty of murder, and over the years she stole thousands of dollars. She's looking at serious prison time. For how long is up to the judge. Meriwether's visiting her now. She may even move to be closer to the prison."

"Did you ever feel bad for not marrying Miss Ruth?"

Gramps looked over the field. "I didn't know what real love was when I gave her that promise ring. We were just kids. I should have called things off much sooner—before she got hurt—but instead I took the coward's way out by just showing up with Tabby." He turned to me. "It doesn't excuse Ruth's actions, but maybe it helps explain them a bit. I don't know."

"How about Earl?"

"Earl, Earl, Earl." Gramps rubbed the back of his neck. "Hiding a body, not reporting a death, obstruction of justice—the list goes on. Either way, he's headed to jail too."

"I'm just glad me and my friends aren't looking at jail time for 'interfering.'"

Gramps chuckled. "I, for one, am glad you interfered. And I'm really glad you and Beau are getting on." He stood and pulled me in for a hug. "Any other questions for me?"

I wiggled away. "Maybe later. Right now, I want to finish my breakfast."

"Boys and food." Gramps followed me inside. "Your daddy nearly ate me out of house and home."

Tick and Mama sat across from each other at the kitchen table, holding hands and talking quietly. Mama looked up and grinned. "Y'all have a good chat?"

"Yes ma'am." I reached for my half-eaten waffle. "Did y'all?"

She pulled her hand away from Tick's and held it out to me. A ring sparkled on her finger. Her face could barely contain the huge smile she gave me. It was something I hadn't seen in a long time. "Oh yeah. We had a good chat."

~~~~~~~

Gran's funeral was at the end of the week. The whole town, minus Miss Ruth, Miss Meriwether, and Earl, showed up to pay their respects. Even Angus came, though his doctor said he had to return to the hospital once the service finished. He'd woken from his coma but still had to spend a couple more days under observation. Beau was going to stay with us until then.

Burma attended the funeral but left straight after to visit

his sister in Texas. Miss Ruth's murder confession had left him reeling, and I think his time away was more to nurse his broken heart than to relax. If a stranger passed through Windy Bottom during the service, they might've mistakenly thought it was one of Burma's loved ones who had died, the way he was carrying on and crying—and, I suppose, in his own way, he *was* mourning the loss of a loved one.

Mama, Tick, and I returned home ahead of Gramps. Mama wanted to give him some time alone at Gran's grave site. Her *proper* grave site, not some hole under a playground slide. Judging from the hidden surface of our kitchen counter, the Windy Bottom Compassion League must've put in overtime. It wasn't until that evening, when things settled down, that I felt I could breathe normal again.

Justice and Liberty came over to toss a ball with Beau and me.

Beau perched on the steps. "So Vidler and your mama are getting hitched, huh?"

"Yep." I threw to Liberty. "It's about time too."

Liberty caught the ball and shook her head before winding up to toss to Justice. "Weddings. They're mushy."

"Maybe," Beau said, "but having Vidler for a dad will have its perks."

"Oh yeah? Like what?" Justice wrapped his mitt around the ball, then threw to me.

I tossed it to Lib.

Beau grinned. "I mean, if we help solve another crime, do you think he'd arrest his *own* kid for interfering?"

I laughed.

Lib threw a knuckleball to Justice.

Beau turned to her. "Sweet arm, Lib."

"Thanks."

Justice looked at his sister. "Did you…did you just…blush?"

"No." She swore and adjusted her ponytail. "And unless you want to experience my umbrage, you'd better watch it."

Justice threw me the ball, then he whipped out his pocket dictionary.

The sun had already sunk below the horizon, but the sky still held on to a pale blue light. A mosquito buzzed by my head, and I swatted it away. It wouldn't be long before cooler weather froze them into nonexistence. But as I looked at my friends in the soft evening glow, I felt all warm inside and full of hope.

Hope that one day Justice wouldn't be a complete moron when it came to vocabulary. And I was pretty confident Beau and I had stumbled onto a path, of some sort, toward becoming friends. I could even hope that Lib—nah, Lib would never willingly wear a dress or give up cursing.

Who we *really* were and who we'd *eventually* become remained to be seen, but I felt pretty sure we'd all be okay.

ACKNOWLEDGMENTS

So many people to thank! First and foremost, my husband, David—you are the king of timelines and catching incongruities. Thank you for setting aside the many hours to help make my work better. My daughter, Jireh, who let me pester her with questions constantly and who showed great patience as I bounced ideas off her. Elenna, thank you for the many hours keeping me company at Starbucks. You are my writing (and coffee) companion. And Nathan, whether you know it or not—you've given my characters many funny conversations.

Thank you also to Sergeant Keith Vidler of the Orange County Sheriff's Office and to John Maxwell of the Winter Springs Police Department for answering all my questions about police and crime scene procedures.

Thank you, Rick Foley, Pharm.D. for putting up with my bizarre questions about various poisons (and for not thinking I was a danger to society)!

And of course a work is never finished until it has gone through the many hands of my fellow Inkstigators: Charlotte Hunter, Leslie Santamaria, Marcea Ustler, Ruth Owen, Jan Eldredge, and Amy Paulshock. This book wouldn't see the light of day if it weren't for y'all. Thank you also to all my Word Weaver friends for your critiques and suggestions.

James Ponti—thank you for taking time to read and help out a fellow author. Your words of encouragement meant the world to me.

And a special thank-you to Kathy Grupe, Reba Gordon, and Kristin Willis for beta reading the early drafts. There's nothing scarier than turning words over to *librarians* for critique!

Last and certainly not least, thank you Sally Apokedak for your patience and thoughtful guidance throughout this book. I am so honored to be able to call you my agent, but even more so to call you my friend.

ABOUT THE AUTHOR

Taryn Souders graduated from the University of North Texas with a specialization in mathematics. She is the author of *Whole-y Cow! Fractions Are Fun*, *How to (Almost) Ruin Your Summer*, and *Dead Possums Are Fair Game*. She lives in Sorrento, Florida, with her family. Visit her at tarynsouders.com.